On impulse, she tried his cell phone once more

Again, the call routed immediately into his voice mail. *Answer your phone, Jared. Where are you?*

A wisp of dark thoughts from the past taunted her. Of a time when rumors had flown about an affair, and whispers had followed in her wake when she walked down the street. Her own sister had begged her to face reality.

Jared had furiously denied the accusations and moved out.

She brushed the painful memories aside. Everything was fine. It had been fine for *years*, and dredging up old hurts never did anyone a bit of good. In the end, she and Jared had reached a truce of sorts, each carefully avoiding those wounds. Each carefully, explicitly explaining daily schedules and destinations in a painfully casual way for months, and just trying to move on.

Trust was such a fragile gift—so easily shattered, so difficult to rebuild. Surely he wouldn't risk destroying what they'd salvaged of their marriage.

Would he?

Dear Reader,

In any relationship, leaving important things unsaid can cause trouble down the road, if not the most painful regrets. Misunderstandings, anger and hurt can deepen when there's too much time to dwell on them. But take that a step further. What if you never had a chance to straighten out a misunderstanding? To tell your boyfriend or husband or child that you're sorry about a mistake you made? Or to say "I love you" one more time?

After writing fifteen books for Harlequin Superromance, I found that the opportunity to write this EVERLASTING LOVE story was a delight. It has been a chance to explore love, caring and emotional issues at a deeper level—between two people who fall in love…and then find that life, with all its love, joy and pain, is just a little more complex than they had expected. I hope you'll enjoy your time with veterinarian Kate Mathers and her husband, Jared.

If you'd like to contact me, you can do so through www.roxannerustand.com or P.O. Box 2550, Cedar Rapids, Iowa 52403. I also blog at www.shoutlife.com/roxannerustand. If you'd like to visit a host of authors who write for Harlequin Superromance, you can find us at www.superauthors.com.

Wishing you all the best,

Roxanne Rustand

SAVE THE LAST DANCE
Roxanne Rustand

HARLEQUIN®

TORONTO • NEW YORK • LONDON
AMSTERDAM • PARIS • SYDNEY • HAMBURG
STOCKHOLM • ATHENS • TOKYO • MILAN • MADRID
PRAGUE • WARSAW • BUDAPEST • AUCKLAND

Recycling programs
for this product may
not exist in your area.

ISBN-13: 978-0-373-71583-1

SAVE THE LAST DANCE

Copyright © 2009 by Roxanne Rustand.

ABOUT THE AUTHOR

Roxanne lives in the country with her family and a menagerie of pets that frequently find their way into her books. If not working at her day job as a registered dietitian, writing at home in her jammies or spending time with her family, you'll find her riding one of the family's horses, playing with her camera or hiding with her nose in a book. She is the author of twenty-three romantic-suspense and heartwarming relationship novels. Her first manuscript won the Romance Writers of America's Golden Heart Award, and her second was a Golden Heart finalist. More recently, one of her books won the *Romantic Times BOOKreviews* award for Best Harlequin Superromance of 2006, and she was nominated for a *Romantic Times BOOKreviews* Career Achievement Award in 2005.

She loves to hear from readers, and can be reached by snail mail at Box 2550, Cedar Rapids, Iowa 52406-2550 or through www.roxannerustand.com.

Books by Roxanne Rustand

HARLEQUIN SUPERROMANCE

As always, to Larry, Andy, Brian and Emily, Andy's beautiful wife, Jenni, and their precious children.

And to my mother, Arline, who has always encouraged my dreams.

CHAPTER ONE

Present Day

ONE THING ABOUT STARTING the day with a burglary—the rest of the day just had to be better.

Dr. Kate Mathers wearily leaned over her desk to close down the computer for the night, turned to grab her purse from a file cabinet drawer and surveyed her office.

This morning it had been in shambles—window glass shattered and scattered across the carpet, papers strewn, her late grandmother's stained glass lamp lying in rainbow shards on her desk. A small figurine of a golden retriever, broken.

Even now, the overhead lights picked out the tiny glittering fragments she'd missed. Precious fragments that brought back such memories…

At least the intruders hadn't bothered the animals in the back rooms, thank God. The veterinary hospital's patients and the boarders were all in roomy cages or pens, and would have been defenseless.

A random act?

Maybe.

The sheriff had certainly supported that theory, though perhaps he had a vested interest in trying to make her believe it.

She fervently hoped he was right, because the alternative was far more frightening. If he was wrong, the threats were escalating. And one day, it wouldn't be just intimidating phone calls and anonymous letters and property damage.

It could become something far more personal.

"You're sure you're okay?" Amy, her twenty-something vet tech, hovered at the door of the office and planted her hands firmly on her slender hips. "I mean, I can stay longer if you don't want to be alone."

An image of the pretty, waiflike blonde as her protector made Kate smile. She waved a hand toward the back door, hoping she looked more confident than she felt. "I'm fine. And I'll be right on your heels, anyway. Casey's plane arrives in less than an hour."

"Cool. Tell her to call me, okay? Maybe we can hang out while she's on break." Hitching the shoulder strap of her purse higher, the girl glanced down the hall. "I locked the front door and checked the windows. Didn't set the security system, though."

"I'll take care of it when I leave, so you can get to your softball game. Thanks again for all your help with the cleanup, by the way."

Amy hesitated, worrying at her lower lip with her teeth, then disappeared. A moment later, the back door creaked open and slammed shut.

Kate took a final walk through the clinic and double-checked the doors and windows, knowing that Amy had taken care of them all, but needing that reassurance. The sheriff had surveyed the damage and taken notes, though his vague promises had done little to dispel her worries.

The lab and pharmacy had been thoroughly ransacked. Dozens of pharmaceutical bottles had been stolen or broken, and the perpetrator had made off with boxes of syringes and needles. A careless thief at that—one who'd left a trail of supplies between the jimmied back door of the clinic and a vehicle waiting in the parking lot.

And now, the idiot was probably shooting up some veterinary drugs that could do him an incredible amount of harm. And if he didn't keel over, he might well be back.

Maybe with friends.

Possibly armed, and certainly dangerous even if he wasn't.

Then again, the perpetrator could have been someone entirely different...bent on reinforcing a warning that her husband, Jared, still refused to heed.

The thought made Kate shudder. How often did Amy stay late, working on the books? Or come in early to feed the animals and clean pens? Casey's former high school classmate still seemed more like a second daughter than an employee, and she wouldn't stand a chance against an intruder. Jared had promised—

With a snort, Kate strode to the back door, locked the shiny new dead bolt, and walked to her black Bravada.

He'd promised to take care of a lot of things this past six months. Estimates on a new security system and steel doors for the clinic, for one thing. Help with the plans to remodel their kitchen at home. Research on hotel and air reservations for the tropical vacation they'd talked about for the past year. The sort of tasks she usually left up to him, because as a lawyer he'd always been much more thorough at gathering and analyzing such information.

But he'd been as busy with his practice as she'd been with hers, and now that he'd also set up a Granite County free legal aid storefront, he had even less time. Late nights, working weekends. When had they last sat down together for a decent supper?

But her clinic couldn't wait any longer. And now with trouble brewing over some of the pro bono cases he'd taken on against powerful local business owners, she was concerned this break-in might be part of a backlash and she needed the security upgrade as soon as possible.

On impulse, she tried his cell phone once more. Again, the call routed immediately into his voice mail. *Answer your phone, Jared. Where are you?*

A wisp of dark thoughts from the past taunted her. Of a time when rumors had flown about an affair, and whispers had followed in her wake when she walked down the street.

Jared had furiously denied the accusations and moved out.

She brushed the painful memories aside. Everything was fine. It had been fine for *years,* and dredging up old hurts never did anyone a bit of good. In the end, she and Jared had reached a truce of sorts, each carefully avoiding past wounds. Each carefully, explicitly explaining daily schedules and destinations in a painfully casual way for months, just trying to move on.

Trust was such a fragile gift—so easily shattered, so difficult to rebuild. Surely he wouldn't risk destroying what they'd salvaged of their marriage.

Would he?

She slid a Jack Johnson CD into the car stereo and settled back for the hour drive to the Madison airport, lifting a hand to wave at familiar faces as she cruised through town.

With just twenty thousand residents and a single vet clinic, many of the Lost River locals were clients, or members of her church, or had served on various PTA committees with her over the years. Small-town connections that warmed her still, even after years of living away from the anonymity of Minneapolis.

The touristy shops and coffee houses on Main Street gave way to the four blocks of grand old homes, then a newer subdivision followed by the grocery, several gas stations and a Pamida discount store. Beyond that, the road curved through meadows and stands of timber on its way out to the four-lane highway leading to Madison.

She smiled, humming along with the music, her heart lifting at the thought of Casey coming home at last after her first year of college. The house would feel alive again, with her daughter's music shaking the rafters and her friends crowding into the family room on Friday nights, the scent of buttery popcorn and warm brownies filling the air.

A small, insistent voice nagged at Kate over the odd catch in Casey's voice during their last phone call, and the long, uneasy silence before she'd insisted it was nothing. She just had a cold. She was…just tired. The reasons spoken with a hesitance that had never been there before.

But maybe she was being truthful. Maybe she *was* tired, needing to come home to just relax before starting her summer job. If there was anything wrong, Casey would've shared it, like always. Wouldn't she?

Four miles down the interstate, Kate topped a low rise. Drew in a sharp breath, and slammed on the brakes. Traffic had been light, but here it was at a standstill—with at least fifty vehicles backed up behind a melee of flashing lights and emergency vehicles. Figures moved rapidly between the patrol cars and two ambulances, then one ambulance took off, made a U-turn across the grass into the north-bound lanes and sped away, its siren screaming.

Five minutes later the other ambulance left. Silently. No lights, no sirens.

And then the traffic started to edge forward,

narrowing to single file on the left-hand shoulder of the road, urged on by a harried officer windmilling his arm.

The crumpled roofline of a partially burned white SUV, a mangled ski rack hanging like tinsel over one edge, was just visible in the opposite ditch as she passed.

It was June. Most outdoors enthusiasts had switched to bike racks by now. *But Jared hadn't, and he drove a white Navigator.*

Kate's heart did a slow-motion somersault in her chest, then settled into place. It couldn't be him. He'd gone to a meeting north of town tonight. The opposite direction. And accidents always happened to someone else. Names in the paper that one didn't recognize, poor souls caught in the wrong place at the wrong time.

But ten minutes later her cell phone rang—a call forwarded by her answering service—and the earth jerked out of its orbit and tumbled crazily into space as she listened. *Jared. A wreck out on the highway just south of town. Get to the hospital as soon as you can.*

But the caller from the hospital couldn't—or wouldn't—give any further details over the phone.

One ambulance had sped back to town on a

hot run. The other one no longer had any need for lights and sirens. Which one had held her husband?

NUMB, HER HEART RACING, Kate pulled to the side of the highway and speed-dialed her friend Deanna, who lived outside of Madison, to ask her to pick up Casey at the airport, then she took a deep, steadying breath and tried Jared's mother, but Sylvia didn't answer.

Kate pulled back onto the highway and took the next exit, then started back to Lost River twenty miles an hour over the speed limit. *It can't be… It can't be.*

Whatever problems they'd had over the years, she'd been sure they would grow old together. Enjoy grandchildren together. Tears burned her eyes as regrets swamped her.

They'd made so many mistakes with each other. Foolish mistakes, though everything had seemed so perfect once upon a time. Surely it couldn't be too late to finally make things right.

He'll be okay. He has to be okay. She gripped the steering wheel tighter to still her shaking hands and forced herself to think back to the time when their future together had been so unexpected, such a bright and special gift….

The Past

"FRAT PARTIES are not my thing," Kate shouted above the blaring, pulsing beat of the latest Tina Turner hit. "So I'm going back to the library."

"Wait—we just got here, and it's almost over, anyway." Deanna, also a sophomore vet student, laughed and dug an elbow in Kate's ribs. "Just look at those guys over there in the corner. I want…the blond one. Red sweatshirt, torn jeans. He is *hot*."

Kate rolled her eyes and started edging backward toward the door, but the crush of bodies gyrating to the music stopped her progress. "This isn't exactly a supermarket, Dee, and I've got a pathology test tomorrow."

"Which you'll ace as always. Why worry?"

"You know why. If my GPA drops, my grant is gone. You'll get your DVM and I'll stay a waitress until I'm too old to carry trays."

"Not hardly, sweetie. C'mon—there's a guy you oughta meet, and I get dibs on the blonde standing next to him." Deanna grabbed Kate's arm and pulled her forward, toward a group of guys in the corner. "Give me five minutes, and you can leave. Promise."

"Right," Kate muttered. She reluctantly followed rather than make a scene in front of far too many sorority girls blessed with good looks, too much money and the ability to deliver a perfect, withering glance at all of the lesser mortals on the planet. *It doesn't matter what anyone thinks,* she reminded herself sharply.

But it did, deep down. In class, wearing cast-off clothes and ratty sneakers, she blended in with most of the other students. But here, glittery dresses and sassy little skirts shimmered and teased, while she'd only been able to pull together black linen slacks and a black sweater from her closet, with a sparkly silver scarf at her throat.

Deanna came to a halt and grinned up at her quarry, her expression at once flirtatious and innocent. Apparently the perfect blend for blondy, because his smile widened as he looked down at her.

They immediately fell into a deep conversation over the upcoming homecoming dance, which gave Kate the perfect chance to escape whatever introduction Deanna had planned. She turned away…and stopped dead.

And stared at quite possibly the most handsome guy she'd ever seen.

He was tall and broad-shouldered, his well-muscled chest straining at the black polo shirt he wore, though he obviously didn't care much about the impression he made. He wore faded jeans and boots, and he'd slung an old leather jacket over his back, suspended by a hooked finger.

Near-black hair brushed the back of his collar and swept away from his face in deep waves, though one rebellious lock hung over his forehead. From his strong, square jaw and high cheekbones to the thick, dark lashes shading his eyes, he had the arresting sort of face that probably stopped most women in their tracks.

But it wasn't his sheer appeal that drew Kate's attention. It was the expression of pure pain in those startling silvery-gray eyes, and that muscle ticking at the side of his jaw.

He was staring down at a surfer-blond woman whose tall, slender body was wrapped in a slinky red cocktail dress. Kate was too far away to hear, but the blonde was clearly talking rapid-fire, with her hands slammed on her hips and her head held at an angry tilt.

She threw a hand up in a gesture of impatience, spun away from him and stalked to the door with her chin up and sparks flashing in her eyes.

With an aching expression, he watched her disappear through the front door, then he went out the French doors to the walled patio. Kate could see him through the window, standing in the moonlight with his hands jammed in his back pockets.

Could he hear the cruel laughter of a trio of sorority girls who were smirking in his direction?

She'd never been a flirt, and even at twenty-one Kate usually just managed awkward blushes and inane remarks if a good-looking guy flirted with her, because she'd grown up determined that nothing—absolutely *nothing*—was going to stand in the way of her future.

Not foolish young boys.

Not reckless passion in the backseat of some guy's car.

Not the early single parenthood and lack of education that had ground her mother's own hopes and dreams to dust.

So Kate had avoided the parties, the silly high school crushes. She'd rarely dated. And in college, she'd practically lived in the library, working hard to ensure that her grants and scholarships would continue.

But all of that resolve faded as she stared at the broad back and bowed head of the man standing out on the patio. She'd always felt soul-deep empathy for animals in pain and people in trouble, and she had no doubt that this was a person who needed a friend.

"Hey, dudes," a deep voice growled into a microphone. "One more song and you're all outta here. Frat rules."

So there wasn't much time. Her heart in her

throat, her palms clammy and her pulse racing, Kate hesitated, then gathered her courage. She crossed the room and stepped out onto the patio.

"Hey, there," she said softly.

"Hey." His voice was low and rich, and sent shivers of awareness dancing across her skin.

He didn't turn around, so she moved to his side and stared up at the stars, too. "I hope I'm not intruding."

"Nope." His mouth lifted in a faint, wry smile. "I suppose you saw the scene inside."

"Um…no." She swallowed hard. "I just thought maybe you'd like to…um, dance. This is the last song of the night."

She'd always been a terrible liar, and he laughed aloud. "You don't need to be kind. Hilary picked quite a place to deliver her little message, but I'll recover."

"I'm sorry if it wasn't a good one."

"It wasn't." He lifted a shoulder. "Then again, sometimes it's better to cut your losses and run— especially if you've made a big mistake. And apparently, she figured she had. With me."

Kate floundered for something intelligent to say, realizing too late that her concern for him had simply made her an unwelcome intruder at a very awkward moment.

"Sorry, I don't think we've met." He looked down at her, a hint of amusement in his faint smile. "I'm Jared Mathers. And you are…?"

Mathers. The late Senator Ellsworth Mathers's son? Heat rose into her cheeks as a dizzying blur of headlines flooded her head. There'd certainly been plenty when Jared entered the University of Minnesota Law School at the beginning of the semester.

The Mathers were millionaires, many times over. Moved in lofty political circles. Shortly before his death last year, the senator had been considered a top contender for the Democratic presidential candidate.

Her first impression of Jared had been miles off. The jacket he carried was Dolce & Gabbana; those faded jeans carried an Armani label, she was sure. And if that wasn't a real Rolex on his wrist, she'd eat the cheap copy she'd bought at a discount store last fall.

No wonder he'd looked amused. She'd pounced on him minutes after the dramatic exit of his girlfriend, looking like a gold digger of the worst kind.

Humiliated, she murmured an awkward excuse and fled, past the supercilious, knowing looks and titters from a gaggle of sorority girls and out to her battered Ford pickup, then home to the cramped apartment over a garage that she shared with Deanna and another vet student.

And hoped she'd never see Jared Mathers again.

SHE SAW HIM the next morning at the vet school library, proving that heartfelt wishes didn't count for much, and that embarrassment wasn't something that dissipated overnight. It was right there, in the heat of her cheeks and the trembling of her stomach, the moment he sauntered over to her, propped his large, tanned hands on the table and flashed an easy grin.

"You didn't leave a slipper at the ball, but your friend Deanna told me you practically live here," he said in a husky whisper. He glanced at the stack of textbooks in front of her, arranged to hide a now-cold cup of coffee and a half-eaten peanut butter sandwich from the eyes of the Nurse Ratched library assistant. "Guess she was right."

"I've got a pathology midterm fourth hour, and a paper due tomorrow." She rearranged the stack of papers in front of her to avoid his eyes, expecting to see a hint of mockery, but when she looked up she found only empathy.

"I hide out in the periodical section of the main library myself," he said. "There's no way I can concentrate at the frat."

His friendly manner was so unexpected that she was once again at a loss for something to say. It almost sounded as if he'd come looking for her, though *that* couldn't be right. *And then she saw what he held in his hand.*

"Oh." Of course he wasn't interested. He'd simply found her pocket-sized planner and was nice enough to return it. "I looked all over for that this morning."

"Must've fallen out of your purse when you left the patio last night. I tried to catch up to you, but you'd disappeared." His eyes twinkled. "If you'd written your address inside, I could've delivered it sooner."

She wondered what he would have thought if he'd seen her aged vehicle or the shabby place where she lived, and breathed a silent thanks for the fact that he'd tracked her down here, in neutral territory. "I can't thank you enough. All of my assignment deadlines and test dates are in there."

"Thank me by having a cup of coffee with me."

"What?"

"I'll buy. Just name the time and place."

"But—"

He laughed. "Just coffee, because I didn't get that last dance, and now I wish I had. Prove your friend wrong, and say yes."

There were a dozen reasons she should decline, but she could well imagine what Deanna had said about her—*hermit* and *recluse* were words her friend bandied about quite often—and Kate's damnable rebellious streak made her nod before she even stopped to think.

"Okay. We could run over to the Student Union, if you don't mind." She flicked a glance at her watch, thankful she had an excuse to make it short. Conversation regarding ovo-parasites, tensile strength of suture material or dystocia in maiden ewes she could handle. What on earth would she have to say to someone like him? "I've got to get back here to book it a while longer before that test, though. Say…just for half an hour?"

He grinned. "More than I'd expected."

They walked toward the redbrick Union, crunching through the dead leaves, breathing in the crisp scent of late fall. She'd figured the situation would be awkward, but the minutes flew as they sat outside on the cement steps of the Union, cradling foam cups of hot coffee and talking casually about random events on campus. He was warm, witty and made keen observations; within minutes she felt as if she'd known him forever.

But then she happened to glance to the east, toward the vet school buildings.

With a start, she looked at her watch and jumped to her feet. "My exam," she exclaimed, tearing down the sidewalk with a quick wave. "I'll be late!"

It wasn't until much later that she realized she'd enjoyed every minute with him, but he'd expertly led the conversation while sharing almost nothing about himself.

A very cool guy.

A dead end.

But what did she expect? He'd undoubtedly realized the obvious—that they couldn't be more different, and that she was totally off the radar as far as his family and peers were concerned.

But it was just as well, she decided over an entire pint of Ben & Jerry's Chocolate Chip Cookie Dough at midnight.

Ice cream was there when you craved emotional support. Men were a complication she just didn't need. Not until she graduated. Not until she set up her own practice and proved to herself that she was secure and a success in her own right.

Next time, Deanna could just try fixing someone else up for a hot date.

CHAPTER TWO

SHE HADN'T GIVEN JARED her address, but at five the next evening he appeared at her door with a fragrant pizza in one hand, plus a grocery sack and a six-pack of Pepsi in the other.

He wore a different pair of disreputable jeans, loafers and that same leather jacket over a dark green sweater, and even in that he could have posed for a Neiman Marcus advertisement.

Though she'd already shucked her dirty coveralls and boots outside, Kate was still in the clothes she'd worn to the stockyards, where she and the rest of her class had practiced bovine pregnancy palpations. But she had to give him credit—he didn't seem to falter at her scraggly ponytail, or the fact that she wore no makeup and had to smell like the wrong end of a cow. "How on earth did you find me?"

"Deanna." His eyes twinkled. "I saw her with you last night, and ran into her in the campus bookstore this morning."

"So she's giving out my address? To just *anyone?*"

"Actually, she dated one of my friends for a while, and we double-dated a few times. I think she'd give me a character reference. She made me promise I wouldn't call you before coming over, because she said you'd just come up with an excuse not to see me." He smiled, and hefted the weight of the pizza box. "Need dinner?"

She wanted to say no, but her stomach growled and the aroma of the pizza made her feel almost dizzy with hunger. "Um…sure. If you'll give me a chance to shower. Come on in."

She stepped aside, avoiding his eyes as he walked in. The clutter was familiar to her—a product of three vet students keeping late hours, with little time for housework—but she could only imagine what someone with live-in maids would think of it.

Deanna and Leesa boarded horses at a stable north of town, so there were bridles hanging from one of the kitchen chairs, and a roping saddle sat on a rack in the corner, with a giant purple bunny propped on its seat.

"Nice rabbit," he said solemnly.

"We all love the state fair, so we spent a lot of time there over Labor Day weekend. I blew my money on corn dogs and minidoughnuts. Leesa couldn't stay away from the carnival games."

He laughed. "Good shot, is she?"

"College marksmanship team, first runner-up. I defy you to find her bed under all of the stuffed animals she won." Kate tossed him the TV remote and waved a hand toward the Formica kitchen table and, beyond that, the swaybacked couch. "Make yourself at home. I'll be out in a minute."

SHE MADE IT BACK IN TEN—feeling infinitely better in clean clothes and a touch of makeup. Miraculously, Jared had found a couple of plates and napkins in the jumbled cupboards, and was now idly lounging in one of the chairs at the table, flipping through her pharmacology textbook.

He looked up with a gleam of appreciation in his eyes. "You sure clean up well. Fast, too. I was betting on an hour. Hungry?"

"Starved." She watched him pull the pizza out of the oven and turn the dial to Off. "I'm still not sure what this is about, though."

He slid a couple of slices of pizza on each plate, then set the rest back in the oven to stay warm. "It's an apology."

"Whatever for?"

"So far, I've been a jerk." He tipped his head

slightly. "I dumped on you at the party, and obviously ruined the night for you, because you left in a hurry. And yesterday I stole all of your study time before that test."

Fragrant steam rose from the spicy pepperoni and thick, gooey mozzarella as she lifted a piece for a first bite. At the explosion of flavor in her mouth, she closed her eyes in sheer ecstasy to savor each nuance. "This is *heaven.*"

"This is Luigi's. Heaven is a few miles farther." He waited until they'd polished off the entire pizza and four cans of soda, then he retrieved a bakery box from the fridge and lifted the lid with a flourish. "Chocolate-raspberry cheesecake, courtesy of the Lincoln Deli."

"Ooooh." She stared at the creamy, otherworldly dessert in awe. "How did you kn—" She caught herself and sighed with bliss. "Deanna."

She served up fat wedges of the cheesecake, but guilt made her stop before taking a first bite. "I didn't leave that frat party because of what you said. I left because…" She swallowed hard. "I was embarrassed. It had to look like I was hitting on you—and right after your girlfriend left. But honest, that wasn't what I intended. And I sure hadn't realized who you were, either."

"Who I was?" His voice took on a sharp edge.

"Oh, right. The *senator's* son. That makes a dif-ference."

"Well…yes."

He pushed away from the table. "I think I'd better be going." His voice was flat, unemotional, but the pain and frustration in his eyes spoke volumes.

"Wait—what did I say?" Mystified, she stared at him. "I think you misunderstood."

"Oh, I understood, all right." He grabbed his jacket from the back of his chair and jerked it on. "I'd thought—I'd hoped—you were different. But it's always the same. It's all about the money. The status."

"You think that it matters to me?" She stared at him, wishing she could take back her words. "I was only trying to be a friend at that party, because your *girlfriend* turned into a banshee in front of all those people. And the only problem with your so-called status was that I thought people might think I was pursuing you *because* of it."

Her voice started rising, but she flat-out didn't care. "Although in retrospect, I really don't give a dang what those shallow sorority twits think about me, anyway."

"You still don't get it." He stopped at the door, one hand on the knob, and looked over his shoulder. "Yeah, there are plenty of people like

Hilary. They come from money, they want more of it, and when it's gone, you may as well just turn to dust for all they care. Six months ago we got engaged. At the frat party? She returned my ring and let me know that she'd found someone else. Who, by the way, belongs to a prominent banking family in Saint Paul. For her, it's all about money."

Kate drew in a breath. "Oh, no."

"And then there are the others, who just assume the worst when they find out about my background. They want nothing to do with someone who will automatically be pretentious, arrogant and shallow." He gave a short laugh. "Sort of a reverse bias, like yours."

Stung, she rose and braced her hands on the table. "Assumptions like that sure must limit your social life."

He shrugged. "Just think about Hilary, and tell me that I'm wrong."

Present Day

KATE MADE THE TRIP to the hospital at roughly the speed of light, trying to concentrate on her college memories and not on what might have been happening in the ambulance far ahead.

She'd arrived to learn that Jared was alive—

though barely. Her staggering relief at that news had sent her buckling into the nearest chair, caught somewhere between joy and fear.

Seconds later, a nurse had hurried over with a clipboard and a million questions about Jared's health, insurance, and whether or not there was a living will or power of attorney in place.

Kate could barely remember her responses, because all she could think about was the constant litany running through her mind. *He's alive... He's alive... He's alive...*

Now, at the sound of hurried, approaching footsteps, she staggered to her feet as a flash of panic rocketed through her. *Doctors...with bad news?*

But it was Cindy Peters, and she wore a sympathetic smile. Dressed in surgical blues and all business, the nurse looked nothing like the sweatshirt-clad gal who'd wrestled a Newfoundland into the vet clinic last week for its annual rabies vaccination.

"Is Jared... Is he okay? Can I see him?"

"I'm sorry, but you can't go back there just yet."

"I want to see my husband," Kate insisted. *"Now."*

"It's been touch-and-go since he arrived. We had to restart his heart a few minutes ago, and we're trying to get him stabilized so he can be taken up to surgery."

"What?" Kate reached blindly for the back of a chair as a wave of cold fear washed through her.

"He lost a lot of blood, Dr. Mathers. I understand he was pinned in the car and it took quite a while to extricate him."

Kate had known that he was in critical condition, but hearing the words slammed that reality home. Numb, she let Cindy guide her back into the chair.

The nurse crouched in front of her and took Kate's hands in her own. "There's an E.R. doctor and a surgeon with him right now, and another surgeon is on the way. As soon as we get the radiology and MRI results, they'll be taking him up to be prepped for surgery."

"Here? Shouldn't he be airlifted somewhere? To a bigger hospital?"

"We have complete facilities here. Two board-certified surgeons. And…" Cindy hesitated. "The main thing is that there just isn't time."

Kate's stomach tied itself into a cold, hard knot. "Tell me about his injuries. I have a right to know."

"Yes, but the doctors need to explain." The nurse's eyes filled with sympathy. "They know you're here, and one of them will be out in a few minutes. What about the rest of your family—are they on the way?"

Kate's heart dropped.

It wasn't hard to read between the lines—there was a good chance Jared wouldn't make it. "I—I called a friend in Madison. She's picking up our daughter at the airport right now. And I called Jared's mother and his sister, but neither answered. The chaplain said he would keep trying them."

"Good, good." Cindy stood and looked across the room at someone, tipped her head toward Kate, then dredged up an encouraging smile. "I need to get back in there. Just hang tight, Dr. Mathers. Your husband has the best of care, and he must be a fighter, or he wouldn't have made it this far."

But a second surgeon was rushing to the hospital. There wasn't time for transfer to a bigger hospital. And Jared's heart had already stopped once.

Kate paced the room. Dropped quarters in a coffee machine and swallowed the bitter brew, barely aware of the scalding heat. Seconds ticked slowly past on the bland white face of the old-fashioned clock above the waiting room door, mocking her rising anxiety. *What could be taking so long? Had Jared already died? Were they waiting for a chaplain to come back to the E.R. to help deliver the news?*

At the sound of footsteps she whirled toward the door.

Ralph Watson, who lived just a mile from their home and who was one of the local internal medicine docs, walked in and took one of her hands in both of his. "I'm glad I was covering the E.R. today, Kate."

The grim expression in his eyes told her more than she wanted to believe.

"I'm taking you back to see him, but he needs to be transferred upstairs right away, because the surgeon is just fifteen minutes out. The anesthesiologist is up there waiting for you, so he can go over the release forms."

He murmured empty reassurances that she could barely hear over the buzzing in her brain. A clammy chill crawled down her back. *Please God, let Jared be all right.*

She lunged out of her chair and followed close at Ralph's heels as he went through the double doors of the E.R. and wound through a maze of curtained cubicles and gurneys to a trauma room at the end. Her heart battered against her ribs and her fear mounted with every step.

Ralph pulled to a stop just outside the door. "Jared is unconscious, but we still take care what we say in hearing distance," he said in a low voice. "He's got a skull fracture and a lacerated liver causing internal bleeding. We might find more problems when we go in. And…" He took a slow breath as he rested a gentle hand on her shoulder.

"He's got some third-degree burns on his legs. This would be a good time for prayer, Kate."

Her knees buckled. The room swam. From somewhere far away, a gentle hand gripped her arm and a voice ordered her to sit down, but she pulled back and blinked hard, forcing away the pinpoints of light sparkling at the edge of her vision. "I'm okay... Just let me see him."

She looked past the doctor's shoulder into the room. An orderly swiftly pulled up the side of the gurney with a clang, while another one gathered the chart and placed it at the foot of the bed.

Oh, God.

Jared was on a ventilator.

On the other side of the bed, a nurse checked the flow rate of a bag of saline hanging from a stand, then pulled a white hospital blanket up over the heavy bandaging on his chest. A framework of some sort held the blankets away from his lower legs.

A monitor beeped and blinked, its glowing green lines tracing the rhythm of his heart.

Kate dealt with emergencies every day. She performed complex surgeries with a high degree of success and far less support staff than surgeons had in a hospital. But seeing Jared here, surrounded by tense staff and a jumble of high-tech hospital equipment, made her feel faint.

She couldn't stifle her sharp cry when the nurse shifted the monitor and its screen came into view.

His pulse was racing, the rhythm irregular.

His oxygen sats were dropping.

He was in shock, and he was getting worse by the second.

The orderlies angled the gurney toward the door and pulled it forward, with the nurse managing the portable electronic equipment and IV stands.

They paused in front of Kate, though she could sense their tension. "Just a second," she whispered.

She took a half step forward and touched Jared's cheek. His face was ashen, with a laceration from cheekbone to jaw, and white bandaging covered his forehead and hair. With every fiber of her being she wanted to hold him. Tell him all the things she should have said long ago. But the grim faces of the staff told her that every moment was critical.

She brushed a kiss against his cheek. "I love you, Jared," she whispered. "I'll be waiting for you." She straightened and watched the gurney rattle away toward the elevator at the far end of the E.R., taking with it a big piece of her heart.

"We'll follow them in the next one," Ralph said, clasping her arm and guiding her to a different elevator. Once inside he rested his hands on her shoulders and looked into her eyes. "Look, I know this is really hard. But I promise you, he's in the best possible hands. Dr. Jacobs spends the school year teaching thoracic surgery out East, but during the summer he lives here. If anyone can pull off a miracle, it's him, and he should arrive any minute."

The elevator door slid silently open at the second floor. Ahead, wide double doors labeled Restricted Access were just swinging shut. To the left, a tall, gaunt man in surgical scrubs—probably the anesthesiologist—stood by a door marked Family Lounge, holding a clipboard. He and Ralph exchanged glances, then he eyed Kate with sympathy.

Overhead, a loud speaker crackled, then blared, *Code Blue! Code Blue! Thirty-four, East Wing. Thirty-four, East Wing.*

A white-faced young nurse burst through the double doors. "He's seizing. Hurry!"

The anesthesiologist and Ralph disappeared into the O.R. Other hospital staff seemed to appear out of nowhere, all racing in the same direction.

The room seemed to fill with glaring light, then went dim at the edges…until Kate remembered to breathe. Jared wouldn't even make it onto the surgical table. He was going to die.

The enormity of this moment, of her overwhelming loss and regret and grief, hit with the force of a freight train. She sank against the wall to the floor and bowed her head.

And began to pray.

CHAPTER THREE

Present Day

SYLVIA MATHERS BRUSHED an imaginary bit of dust from her classic black Yves Saint Laurent coat-dress, fixed a haughty smile on her face and strolled into the restaurant, well aware that she radiated Old Money to those seated at the tables.

As well she should.

The décolleté V of the lapels framed a string of perfect, creamy pearls inherited from Ellsworth's mother, and the vintage couture dress itself was a wise purchase made in the eighties that would never go out of style. She hadn't dared tell Ellsworth about this particular price tag—though back then, money had been of little consequence and image had been everything.

Image and political alliances and the illusion of class that had lured even more benefactors into her late husband's fold during his political campaigns.

Not bad for a barefoot girl born to dirt-poor Oklahoma farmers who'd had too many kids, too many bills and little regard for education.

She'd been the first to break the mold. After scrabbling her way through college, she'd made sure she found the right jobs, where she could meet the right people. Now, very few remembered that she'd ever been the young, sexy executive secretary in Senator Mathers's office who had helped end his first marriage, because she'd carefully cut those unfortunate little complications from her address book the day after her own marriage to Ellsworth.

Nanette Laughton set aside her water glass and lifted a brow at Sylvia's approach. "My, you're early, dear."

"A rare thing, I know. I went to the health club first, then the standing appointment with my hairdresser. Georgio was right on schedule today."

Sylvia settled into a ruby velvet chair opposite her friend, only slightly miffed at Nanette's choice of position at the table. Early-evening sunlight filtered through the curtains at her friend's back, highlighting her platinum blond hair and casting her face in subdued, ambient lighting.

Sylvia, facing the low angle of the sun, knew it accented every wrinkle and line on her own face.

She usually took care to avoid the direct and unflattering lighting. "I'm so glad we were able to meet here for dinner. I haven't been to Stillwater in years."

"And it's such a lovely drive over here from the Twin Cities. We should do this more often."

After the waitress took their orders, Nanette leaned a little closer and lowered her voice to a whisper. "You're lovelier than ever, by the way. I just knew Dr. Falk would do a wonderful job for you." She touched a fingertip to the smooth outside corner of her eye. "I know I couldn't have been happier."

Sylvia managed a faint smile, though her stomach twisted into a nervous knot as she thought about the money she'd spent and the stock she'd had to sell off last month.

Life was still all about packaging, really… keeping up appearances, contacts and the impression that all was well, even though the family's software company had gone belly-up years ago, amidst allegations of upper-level corruption and mismanagement. Downturns in the stock market had decimated what was left. The senator had died soon afterward while under a cloud of suspicion about his personal life.

He'd certainly chosen an unfortunate time to die, given the family's financial disaster and the fact that Jared was just starting college.

But now, with Julia left to marry off, Sylvia had a last chance to make the right connections for one of her children.

Sylvia had counted on Jared. Tutored him. Worked at carefully managing the right introductions so he could marry well and provide his mother and sister with the elegant, comfortable lifestyle they deserved.

Sylvia's modest stock portfolio and rigid attention to the market had kept them afloat, but even now, twenty years later, Jared's selfishness burned.

Maybe his tacky little wife had lured him into an unfortunate marriage all those years ago, but this time, with Julia, Sylvia wasn't going to let *anything* go wrong.

Nanette took a delicate sip of her raspberry iced tea. "And how is your daughter?"

"She's still out East, but she's nearly done with her thesis. After that, well…" Sylvia made a graceful, offhand motion with her fingertips, carefully dismissing the years Julia had spent trying to "find herself" in college. "She's still thinking about medical school or a Ph.D. in biology. And your son?"

"Robert's still leaning toward family practice." Nanette shook her head, obviously distressed. "I keep telling him that plastic surgery is the way to go, with all the baby boomers sliding into old age, but he says he'd rather work with the disadvantaged. Can you imagine? I'm sure he'll come to his senses, though…once he finds the right woman and settles down. He has no idea how much it costs to raise a family these days."

The perfect opening. "So true. Those responsibilities do bring things into focus." Sylvia idly toyed with a mandarin orange in her salad. "Our children seem so alike."

"Perhaps we can try arranging another meeting. They seemed to like each other rather well at the club on the Fourth of July."

The Laughtons were an old, moneyed family, with a sprawling estate on Lake Minnetonka and a palatial home on a cliff overlooking Lake Superior. The possible connection was definitely enticing.

Sylvia imagined Robert and Julia living on an equally grand estate with a pleasant little mother-in-law cottage, and urging Sylvia to move there. The vision filled her with a sense of warmth and security she hadn't felt in a long time. "That would be lovely. I can just imagine—"

From inside Sylvia's vintage Gucci handbag came the soft trill of her cell phone. She swiftly reached into the bag, glanced at the caller ID on the screen and pressed a side button to mute the ring, irritated at the interruption. Whatever Kate had to say, she could certainly leave it as voice mail.

Sylvia had noticed three other messages when she walked out of the salon—calls she'd missed due to the constant chatter and the noise of hair dryers. She'd simply have to catch up on all of them later.

Nothing was as important as this conversation with her friend.

"Sorry. As I was saying, just imagine our two together." Sylvia gave Nanette a conspiratorial smile. "Wouldn't Robert and Julia give us the most adorable grandchildren?"

THE VISION of Jared's ashen, damaged face kept crowding into Kate's thoughts as she sat curled up at one end of a couch in the waiting area by the operating room. The television was blaring in the corner, but she had no idea what the newscasters were saying.

The longing to touch Jared, to talk to him, welled up inside her, her emotions swinging between hope and fear as she fought to stay in control.

Two other families had filed in, settled down to wait, then left—one overjoyed, the other overwhelmed with sorrow. And still, there'd been no word about Jared since the anesthesiologist had come out with his release forms.

Jared had suffered that second cardiac arrest just inside the O.R., but he'd rallied and had now been in surgery for almost an hour. An hour that seemed like a lifetime, marked by the inexorable ticking of the second hand on the clock.

Tick.

Tick.

Tick.

Kate's fingers itched, flexing involuntarily as she imagined holding the same surgical instruments. She remembered the broken hips and backs and legs she'd operated on—snaking rods up through the marrow on femurs and tibiae; using screws and pins and wires to draw fractured shards together into a solid, functional structure.

But it was her husband on the other side of those double doors…the father of her daughter, the man who'd been a part of her life all these years. It was still almost impossible to wrap her mind around the thought that any moment could be his last, and there was nothing she could do about it.

"Dr. Mathers?"

She swallowed hard against the fear rising in her throat and looked up to see a somber chaplain with an equally grim-faced nurse at his side. Her heart stuttered. "Jared—"

"Oh, my dear," the elderly gentleman said

quickly. "We didn't come with bad news. As far as we know, he's still weathering surgery very well. How are you holding up through all of this?"

Kate looked down at her knotted hands and willed herself to relax. "I wish our daughter was here… I haven't heard a word from her yet. Has anyone been able to reach Jared's mother or sister?"

"We've left several messages for his mother, but we did reach his sister, Julia," the nurse told her. "She's trying to arrange a flight home from New York." The woman pulled a slip of paper from her pocket. "Also, the receptionist in the E.R. took a message from a friend of yours. Deanna, is it?" She unfolded the note. "Your daughter's plane was held up in Denver due to bad weather, so she missed her connection from Minneapolis to Madison. The next open seats wouldn't get her to Madison until late tomorrow afternoon."

"Oh, no," Kate breathed. She imagined Casey trying to find a shuttle to a hotel, or simply camping out in the airport for the night. Either way she was all alone, a young college student who felt independent but who'd always be Kate's baby. And she'd be so devastated if she didn't have a chance to say goodbye….

The staggering thought blindsided Kate, sending a gut-deep wave of grief rushing through her.

"But your friend and her husband are already driving to Minneapolis to get her," the nurse continued. "They figure they'll make it back here by early morning." She handed over the note, the handwriting nearly illegible. "I thought I'd better decode Marie's handwriting for you."

When the nurse's voice finally registered, Kate sagged against the back of her chair in relief. "Thank God."

The two staff members exchanged awkward glances, then pulled up a couple of chairs to face Kate's and sat down.

The chaplain's brow furrowed as he reached out to take her hand. "There's something else, dear. The sheriff wants to talk to you, but we asked him to wait until after your husband is out of surgery."

"Why? He wants to deliver a *ticket?*"

"It's regarding the other person in your husband's car."

"Who?"

"The deceased."

"What?"

"You didn't know?" The chaplain frowned and looked at the nurse, but she lifted a shoulder and shook her head in response. "I'm so very sorry if this person was a friend or relative, Dr. Mathers."

"Someone was with him?" Kate thought back

to when she'd called the law office, after Jared didn't answer his cell.

Tom had said Jared was on his way north to a meeting, so Tom couldn't have been in the car, and their legal secretary was on a Canadian fishing vacation this week. There'd been no mention of anyone else.

And Jared had been found on a road going south out of town, not north.

"Your husband was extricated just in time, but the other person was badly tangled in the wreckage and was dead at the scene. The EMTs and officers weren't able to get her out fast enough, and the body was badly burned."

Kate's stomach roiled at the thought. *That could have happened to Jared, too.* Guilt followed her flash of relief. Her husband had been spared, but another family would be facing a terrible loss.

"She appeared to be a young woman," the chaplain continued. "Slender. The investigators will need to use dental records for a positive identification, but it would save them time if you knew who she might be."

Young. Slender.

The old, nagging uncertainty, dormant for so many years, flared to life. The late nights…the working weekends… Did this add up to a situation she'd never imagined facing again?

But just as quickly, Kate tried to extinguish her doubts.

"I…really have no idea who she is. Call Tom Williams, my husband's law partner." She rattled off Tom's cell phone number. "She was probably a client."

The chaplain jotted down the number. "I'm sure that must be the case," he murmured. He handed the slip of paper to the nurse, who then left the room. "I hope that's all the sheriff needs. If not, he may be calling on you later."

"Of course." Kate eyed the clock, willing the minute hand to move faster. Saying yet another silent prayer for Jared and the surgeons who were working to save his life. She tried to imagine what was happening right now, wishing desperately that someone would come out to tell her.

"I'll be glad to sit with you for a while." The chaplain's soft voice broke through her thoughts. "This isn't a time to be alone."

His sad eyes and drooping jowls reminded her of a geriatric basset, and the weariness in his voice spoke of too many hours at the hospital as it was.

"You must have been here on overtime today, and I'm fine. Really." She dredged up a smile.

"I'll try my mother-in-law's phone every few minutes, and I know she'll be here with me as soon as she hears the news."

"Well…"

"Please, do go. Honestly, the solitude is peaceful."

The old man led her in a prayer for Jared and his loved ones, then rose and clasped her hands in his. "If anything changes, have a nurse call me. I can be back in fifteen minutes."

If anything changes.

Translated… If your husband dies. The enormity of it settled over her like a heavy mantle, making it hard to breathe.

"Thanks so much." She nodded in farewell, slumping back in her chair after he left. She sat for a moment, then jumped to her feet and started to pace. Back and forth in the waiting room. Down the hall to the elevators, then back again, trying to settle the jitters in her stomach.

Every time she saw a nurse in the hallway she froze, half-afraid the person was coming to deliver bad news.

And every few minutes, she tried speed-dialing Jared's mother.

At nine forty-five, Sylvia finally picked up with a terse, "Yes?"

Her irritable response changed to stunned

silence, then near-hysterical tears when Kate gently explained the situation.

"I was just heading back to the Twin Cities from Stillwater." Sylvia's voice shook. "I'll turn around at the next exit."

"You're almost three hours away. It's late. Is there anyone you can call to come with you?"

"I—I don't think so. But I can get there just a little after midnight if I push the speed limit. Call me if *anything* changes... And if you hear any news at all about his condition, I want to know it."

"Sylvia—"

"I'll be there as soon as I can." The connection ended.

Kate stared at her phone for a moment, Sylvia's tense voice still ringing in her ear, then she pocketed the phone and resumed her pacing.

"Dr. Mathers?" A deep baritone voice reverberated down the hall.

"That's me." She spun around to find a man in surgical scrubs, a mask dangling from his neck, standing just outside the double doors of the operating room. She hurried over to him. "Tell me— how is Jared doing?"

"We're still trying to repair the damage to Jared's chest and liver. There's far more than we could see on the MRI, and we haven't been able to stop the internal bleeding thus far." The man's deeply lined face revealed no glimmer of optimism. "He's coded twice already, and the situation is grave. I'm so sorry."

Kate felt herself go cold, clammy. The room grew dim as she focused desperately on the surgeon's face. "B-but there's still a chance. Once the surgery is over."

"He's on life support, and he's in God's hands, Dr. Mathers. I can't rule out another crisis that could seriously affect his quality of life—or end it." He took a deep breath. "But right now, decisions need to be made and they need to be made fast. Just how well do you know your husband's wishes?"

She closed her eyes as a wave of memories assaulted her. Oh, once she'd known his wishes very well—he'd been closer to her than the beat of her own heart. But their troubles, so many, these past few years, had created a chasm that neither had been able to cross.

So how well did she know him now?

CHAPTER FOUR

The Past

"I SAW YOUR BOYFRIEND at the library last night," Deanna teased. "I think he was looking for you."

Kate's heart fluttered, and she exhaled slowly, trying to keep her expression blank. "I'm not sure who you mean."

Deanna rolled her eyes. "Right. A guy like Jared Mathers is certainly forgettable—if you're ninety and have serious dementia."

"He isn't my boyfriend. I barely know the guy." Kate turned another page of her radiology textbook and uncapped her yellow highlighter, trying to ignore the image of him that had been sliding into her thoughts all day.

The sexy gleam of straight white teeth when he flashed a smile that warmed her clear to her toes.

The lazy grin that deepened the dimples bracketing his sensual mouth. The sensual slide of his silver-eyed gaze, shaded by long, thick eyelashes any girl would kill for. Money. Status. Looks that ought to grace some glossy advertisement in an outdoorsman's magazine, though he had none of the self-absorption of some of the rich pretty boys on campus.

So totally out of her league that she really, *really* needed to forget she'd ever met him. "I talked to him for a few minutes at a party. Then I ran into him by accident at the library, and… well…we had that pizza…"

"Sounds like a good start to me."

"And the end. That was two weeks ago and I haven't seen him since."

Deanna shrugged. "Well, I'd swear he was looking for you. In a casual, offhand sort of way."

"Maybe he was just lost."

"A couple girls went up and talked to him—all that coy, flirtatious stuff, you know?" Deanna snorted. "He certainly could've asked them for directions, but he didn't give 'em a second glance."

Hope and longing warred in Kate's chest, coupled with a healthy dose of reality. She slapped her textbook shut. "Look, there's no point in talking about this, okay? Have you *seen* his family on the front page of the newspaper? Do you know who his dad was? Who his uncles are? Maybe he goes out slumming now and then, but I won't be some rich boy's amusement, and he sure as heck wouldn't *really* be interested in me. Like I said, end of story."

"Only if you want to throw away a once-in-a-lifetime chance. I don't mean the money—I just mean he seems like a really nice dude. You're crazy not to see that."

The incredulity in Deanna's eyes nearly made Kate laugh. "Does 'worlds apart' mean anything to you?"

"What are we in, the dark ages? You're not exactly some peasant."

"I would never fit in his world, and I have no illusions about that." Turning away to hide her emotions, Kate closed her eyes briefly, remembering the mocking glances of the sorority girls when she'd tried to console Jared the night his girlfriend jilted him. "Can you see me on his arm at some governor's ball? Making conversation with political types or discussing my exhausting yoga, golf and tennis schedule with a gaggle of women who live for that sort of thing?"

Deanna shrugged. "I'm just saying that you ought to give the guy a chance."

Kate bit back her rising frustration. "I'm sure he really doesn't want one. And even if he did, nothing matters more to me than school right now. I barely have time to eat, much less have a social life."

"I already told him you'd say that."

Kate whirled around to look at her. "You talked to him? I thought you said you saw him from across the room, or something."

An unrepentant grin lit Deanna's eyes. "I know how much you love my interference, so I was trying to skip over that minor detail. Here, he gave me something for you." She pulled a scrap of paper from her pocket and slid it across the table. "I guess we should get an answering machine. He told me he's tried to call several times, but there's never an answer. So if you'd like to meet him for coffee sometime, here's his number."

Suppressing the urge to snatch it up, Kate gave the piece of paper an offhand glance. "Someday, maybe."

"You could borrow something to wear, if you want." Deanna studied her for a long moment. "My mauve gauzy top and black silk slacks would look great on you."

"Deanna."

Her friend held up both hands, palms up. "Okay, okay. I'm done with being fairy godmother, I promise." Shouldering her backpack, she started for the door. "I'm heading over to check on how my surgery dog's doing. Want to come along? We could stop at Bill's Pizza."

Kate's stomach rumbled at the suggestion but she shook her head. "Can't."

Deanna hesitated in the open doorway of the kitchen, resting one hand on the frame to look back. "I think you'll regret not taking a chance, Katy. When something really wonderful comes along, you've got to be brave enough to go for it."

Long after her friend was gone, Kate stared at the closed door. Brave…or just plain foolish?

Like always, she would follow her head and not her heart, because she knew which way would lead to the ruin of her dreams. Her future. Everything she had worked for since that fateful day in eighth grade when her future had changed forever.

She only had to remember her mother's tragic life to keep things in perspective.

SOLID PLANS and absolute focus melted into a puddle beneath her feet when Kate walked into the corner grocery at Elm and Sixth the next day and found Jared kneeling in front of a little boy with tear-streaked cheeks not more than three or four years old.

Behind them, a middle-aged man in a white

apron bent over a broom and dustpan, sweeping up shards of broken glass.

A surly woman with a tangle of long, brassy hair gripped the boy's hand and fixed Jared with a challenging glare. "So what are you gonna do about it, college boy? You got thirty dollars?"

The little boy twisted within her iron grasp to look up at her, his cheeks streaked with tears and his mouth trembling. The fear in his eyes made Kate want to gather him up in her arms and run for the nearest child protection agency.

"It was my fault, not the boy's," Jared said evenly. Only his white-knuckled grip on his car keys betrayed his tension. "I'll be responsible for the cost." His gaze flicked to the boldly lettered sign above an open display case of horse and dog figurines that read, YOU BREAK IT, IT'S YOURS!

"You heard the college kid," the woman snarled, yanking on the child's arm as she started for the door. "He's the one who broke it, and he's the one paying."

Kate stepped aside so the woman could sweep past her. "Just take it easy on your son, ma'am," Jared said. "He didn't do anything wrong."

The woman glanced back over her shoulder, her expression stormy and her mouth opening for another retort. When her eyes met Jared's, she snapped her mouth shut and her stride faltered, then she disappeared out into the night.

Kate did a double take at the lethal expression in Jared's eyes. He was *angry* on behalf of the defenseless child, and she suddenly knew that it had been curious small hands that had dropped the figurine. Jared had jumped to the boy's defense to save him from his mother's wrath.

And right there, in the doorway of Mel's Grocery, Kate felt her heart tumble out and land at her feet.

Jared stood up in one fluid motion, nodded to acknowledge her and turned to the storekeeper. "I've got ten on me right now. Can I sign an I.O.U. for the balance?"

"And I'd see you again when?" The older man gave him a knowing look. "I'll take a credit card for the rest."

"Can I work it off? Just tell me what to do, and I'll be here."

If he'd said that he had purple elephants waiting outside, Kate couldn't have been more surprised. Surely he carried a handful of credit cards with sky-high limits and had an endless flow of family money.

Jared's cheeks turned ruddy. He stepped closer to the man and lowered his voice to say something, then he slipped off his watch and handed it over. "I'll be back, just as I said. Tomorrow evening and the night after that. This is for security."

He gave Kate a quick, embarrassed glance as he turned on his heel and headed for the door. Only after he was gone did she remember to snap her mouth shut. Jared Mathers, son of a state senator, was going to work off his debt in a dreary little corner grocery?

She grabbed a frozen pizza from the case and took it to the front of the store, fished a five-dollar bill from her pocket, and cleared her throat to catch the attention of the clerk.

He set aside his broom and rounded the counter wearing the watch Jared had given him, a smirk on his beefy face. "Dumb kid," he muttered, glancing at his wrist. "You know him?"

"A—a little."

"He thinks I fell for it, but what would some college kid be doing with a Rolex? It's gotta be a street corner knockoff. If he doesn't come back I'll call the cops. I *never* forget a face and name."

She stared at the gleaming watch. Expensive watches had never been a part of her world, but if this was a knockoff, it had to be an incredible copy. "Jared is an honorable guy. He'll do whatever he promised to do."

The man snorted as he rang up the pizza. "Well,

you tell pretty boy that he'd better, if he knows what's good for him. I won't hesitate to press charges. Hear?"

A shiver of worry crawled through her. What would that do to Jared's goal to enter law?

She'd misplaced the small scrap of paper with his phone number, and he was probably unlisted. He likely had a private condo in some exclusive area near the campus…unreachable by the likes of her.

"I—I don't know where he lives, honest." Scooping up her change and the pizza, she hurried to the door. "I'll tell him if I see him, though."

Outside, she scanned the darkened street. Could he still be close by? Her heart lifted at the possibility. She'd have a chance to relay the message, then maybe they'd talk awhile. Though a small, inner voice reminded her that they couldn't be more different, the thought of his smoky silver gaze and deep laughter warmed her clear to her toes despite the crisp October chill in the air.

A half-dozen college girls ambled down the sidewalk together, each with a backpack slung over one shoulder, laughing. Across the street, a young couple walked hand in hand through a drift of autumn leaves.

But Jared was nowhere to be seen.

KATE LOOKED FOR HIM on campus the following day, then asked Deanna and several friends if they knew where he lived. No one seemed to know anything about him, the college refused to release contact information, and there were no phone book listings that were even close.

Finally—as a last resort—she crossed the commons in front of the Student Union and intercepted two of the girls she'd seen at the party where she'd first met him. Oblivious, they swept past her, deep in conversation over some gaffe by a fellow sorority member.

"Wait—please," Kate called after them.

They turned as one and stared at her faded jeans and medical pullover smock emblazoned with the vet school logo, each with a single eyebrow raised in elegant disbelief at the intrusion.

If Kate hadn't needed to talk to them, she would've rolled her eyes at their clonelike supercilious air and gone on her way.

"You…*need* something?" the tall blonde asked, glancing at her watch.

"I saw you. At the fraternity party a few weeks ago. And…um… Jared Mathers was there."

"*You're* the one who was chasing him after Hilary dumped him!" She gave her friend a triumphant look. "See? I told you. Hilary was livid when she heard about it."

"Why would she care if she dumped him?" Kate felt her face warm. "He looked upset. I just went over to talk to him."

The two girls exchanged glances, then the shorter one snickered. "R-i-i-ght. Not like he'd be a target for every last gold digger on campus, or anything."

The temptation to fire back a sharp retort nearly consumed Kate. "I just need to tell him something," she said evenly. "Today. Would you know where I can find him?"

"Believe me, sugar, you don't stand a chance, so don't waste your time." She glanced above Kate's shoulder, and her eyes lit with amusement. "The Mathers family would see to that. Right, Jared?"

Laughing, the two girls strolled away.

Kate felt the warmth in her cheeks turn to fire as she slowly turned and found Jared dismounting from a sleek ten-speed not more than three feet away. He'd probably heard every last word.

She froze, unable to speak, wishing she could simply die right on the spot.

But instead of finding disgust or mockery in his eyes, she only found sympathy, and embarrassment that nearly matched her own. "I...wasn't trying to find you so I could hit on you or anything," she managed after an awkward pause.

"I know," he said wryly. "You've made that pretty clear."

"I mean, you seem like a great guy and everything. I'm just not really looking right now, with school and my job and homework and all. I—" *Babbling. I'm totally babbling here. Really cool, Kate.*

She took a deep breath to steady herself, then caught a glimmer of a smile tilting his mouth. "I'm sorry. I don't usually run on like that. What I needed to tell you was that guy at the store plans to press charges if you don't show up tonight to pay for the merchandise or work it off."

His smile faded. "I plan to be there, just as I said."

"He sure doesn't think so."

"Then I guess he'll be surprised." Jared's gaze slid away, toward the Walker Chemistry Building. "He's got a brand-new employee for the next two nights. I gave him my word, along with my watch."

Surprised, Kate studied his profile. The set of his strong jaw suggested that he possessed a lot more backbone than she'd expected in a pampered rich boy, though the tick of a small muscle in his cheek betrayed his stress.

"Um…do you, like, need a loan or anything?"

It was probably a foolish question, yet something wasn't right here. Maybe he'd blown his fancy allowance from home.

He gave her a startled look. "A loan? I...pay my debts on my own. But it was nice of you to offer."

"You could pay me back." The sooner the better, or there'd be no groceries on her table this week or next. But from the decisive shake of his head that wouldn't be an issue. "I guess that's a 'no'?"

His faint smile returned. "Right."

The look of stubborn pride on his face conveyed far more than his words, echoing the same kind of determination she'd developed herself over the years. She had no right to pry into his personal affairs, and once again, she felt her admiration and curiosity deepen, coupled with an unexpected sense of connection.

And maybe he felt it, too, because he tipped his head and studied her, his eyes warm and deep and compelling, as if he were seeing into her very soul. "You aren't like any girl I've ever met," he said finally.

A little embarrassed, she ducked her head. "Understatement of the year?"

"No—I mean it." He held her gaze with his. "Go out with me Friday night. Please?"

A flash of panic hit her. "I can't."

"Saturday?"

"Sorry. Really—I have to work all weekend. And I've got a ton of homework, and…"

"Please?"

His voice lowered, and the note of vulnerability won her over when nothing else would have. "Well…"

"Nothing fancy… Maybe a movie at the dollar theater? Pizza?"

He was all wrong for her. She'd been down this road before, and it had led to heartbreak and humiliation because of who she was and where she'd come from. But she suddenly knew that if she didn't grab this chance, she'd regret it for the rest of her life. What could be the harm with just one simple date?

"Saturday, then? But it would have to be after nine."

"Deal. I'll pick you up at your place, nine sharp." He climbed onto his bike and grinned at her. "Don't forget."

She watched him disappear across the campus and felt her heart turn to lead. Just talking to him did funny things to her insides.

Made her imagine things that couldn't be.

Made her temporarily forget why any relationship—especially with someone who would have so much to lose—was impossible.

Nope, she wouldn't forget.

But between now and Saturday night, she was going to think up a perfect excuse....

Or maybe she'd tell him the truth.

CHAPTER FIVE

KATE'S RESOLVE VANISHED when Jared appeared at her door at nine o'clock Saturday, with a tentative smile and two tickets for a campus production of *Much Ado About Nothing,* starting at nine-thirty. He was dressed in khakis and a black polo shirt that emphasized his broad chest and biceps. Just looking at him nearly took her breath away.

He stared down at her, his eyes darkening and his smile fading. "You are," he said quietly, "the most intriguing person I've ever met. I thought I'd find a note on the door saying that you couldn't go."

She bit back a laugh. "Actually, I wrote one, but tore it up a few minutes ago."

From somewhere back in the apartment, Deanna called out, "I made her do it, so you can thank me."

Startled, he looked over her head toward the sound of Dee's voice, then touched Kate's cheek with his fingertips. "Look, if you don't want to go, just say the word."

He was so different from what she would've expected of someone with a background like his. Where was the superficial charm, the arrogant, offhand sense of entitlement that so many of the fraternity guys wore like a badge of honor?

Remembering his gentle defense of the little boy at the corner store, she fought the urge to lean into his touch. *One date. What could be the harm? Just one evening, and she'd back away from all the temptation before her...before it was too late.*

"That note was...um...a mistake," she admitted.

"I'm glad." His eyes twinkled. "Tell your friend that I owe her a favor. Are you all set?"

She grabbed her purse and denim jacket from a bench by the door. Out in the crisp night air, their hands automatically caught and held as they strolled through the fallen leaves covering the sidewalks.

The sweet scent of burning leaves drifted on the breeze, coupled with the aroma of cinnamon-laden apple pie emanating from one of the 1940s stucco bungalows they passed on their way to the campus theater.

"I hardly know you," Jared said, "yet I feel like I've known you forever. Is that weird?"

She angled a teasing glance at him. "Maybe we were siblings in another life."

He laughed. "Believe me, I don't think of you

as my sister." Silvery moonlight painted the campus in shimmering, eerie shades of gray. In the shadows of a massive old oak, he stopped and turned to her, lifting her chin gently. "In fact, I've wanted to do this since the moment we met."

He hesitated, giving her a chance to pull away, then lowered his mouth to hers for a brief kiss.

It was as if she'd been touched with fire. Sensation and longing spread through her, and she reached up to wrap her arms around his neck. "One more?"

This time, he kissed her longer—still chaste, still holding back, but in that kiss she felt such connection, such desire unfolding inside her, that at first she was only dimly aware of the single word echoing through her heart.

Forever... Forever...

And she knew that no matter what happened in her life, no matter what happened with this relationship or with any others, she would never forget this moment in Jared's arms.

THE IRONY OF THE PLAY'S romantic conflicts amused her, though she scarcely heard the actors speak. Instead, she was aware of Jared's woodsy aftershave. The warmth of his arm next to hers. The surreptitious glances of some of the other students in the theater.

For this one precious night, she felt like the wealthiest princess in the world—flying high and savoring every moment.

Afterward, they lingered at a coffee shop, talking until the lone waitress stopped mopping the floor and told them it was long past time for the place to close.

With obvious regret, Jared stood, flipped a five-dollar bill onto the table and ushered Kate outside. "I think I could've stayed there till dawn, if she hadn't told us to go. Next time, we'll have to try that all-night diner on Fourth."

Next time? *Maybe...* Kate's heart lifted, even as reality started to nip at her thoughts. "What would your mother say, if she knew you were hanging out with someone like me?"

"Like you?" The surprise in his voice was palpable. "What wouldn't she like?"

"Who have you dated before—girls from your country club? Your social circle?"

"Yes, but..." He faltered. "That's just 'cause they were attending the same school, I guess."

"I don't think we should see each other again."

At that, he stopped short and gently swung her around to face him. "My family has nothing to do with this."

"No?" She took a slow breath as she gathered

her courage. "Mine does…and I think yours would take issue with that."

"Our families don't matter."

They would. He just didn't know it yet, and if she could save them the embarrassment and awkwardness of that revelation, they'd both be better off.

But then their eyes met. Locked.

Looking up into his strong, chiseled face, she saw his eyes melt as he stared down at her, and her heart expanded until it barely fit in her chest.

She'd dated a few boys in high school. She'd had a girlish attraction to some of the coolest guys at school, and after seeing the *Star Wars* and *Indiana Jones* movies, she'd had a silly crush on Harrison Ford.

But never had anyone made her feel like Jared did—a soul-deep attraction that she felt with every fiber of her being.

"I want to see you again. Tomorrow night?"

The deep timbre of his voice and its absolute determination sensitized her skin, sending renewed shivers of awareness through her. Every bit of her resolve fled like a fallen leaf on the rising October wind.

She nodded, feeling a little faint.

The obstacles between Shakespeare's young lovers in the play had been amusing…but they didn't hold a candle to what lay in her past. *One more time…just one more evening couldn't hurt, could it?*

But all the way home she prayed that she hadn't made a big mistake.

SHE SPENT SUNDAY AFTERNOON in the vet school library, trying to study for her anatomy test on Monday. Mostly, she watched the time tick by slowly…slowly…slowly…taunting her with the imperceptible drag of the minute hand as it made its way around the broad white face of the clock on the wall.

At five, she allowed herself to launch out of her chair and jog home, where she showered, tried on four different outfits, and finally made a cheap box of macaroni and cheese to share with Deanna. Leesa, as usual, was at the stable, where she'd go whenever she had a spare hour or two.

"Hot date," Deanna mused, a forkful of garish orange macaroni halfway to her mouth. "Hmm. I wonder who it could be."

Kate fixed her with a quelling stare. "Don't embarrass me when he comes over, okay?"

Her hand at her chest, Deanna feigned astonishment. "Me? Embarrass you? Never."

"I shouldn't even be doing this, you know."

"Why not? Jared is an absolute doll. From the

look in his eyes, he already adores you. What's not to like?"

"Charlesburg."

At the single word, Deanna lowered her fork to her plate, and her other hand dropped to her lap.

"See?" A wave of hopelessness and frustration settled in Kate's stomach like a cold, dead weight. "I have to tell him, because he'll find out anyway. Either way…"

"But you aren't responsible for your family. No one can hold that against you."

"Headline news? Of course they can. Think 'high school prom.'"

Whenever she thought of that night, the embarrassment still sent flames burning in her cheeks.

Because she lived so far out in the country, she'd offered to drive into town and meet her date at the school. Phillip had been inside, standing in a circle of friends, their heads bent together. When one of them spied her, they'd broken apart instantly and her heart had done a slow-motion dive to the floor.

Phillip turned his back on her, took the arm of Chelsea Goodwin and went out on the dance floor. Two of his friends strolled over to meet Kate, their faint smirks barely hiding their anticipation.

"Is it true?" Wendy exclaimed. "Really, really true?"

Kate stared at them, feeling herself shrink against the cool cement block wall of the gym.

"I mean, I never met anyone related to a *murderer* before!"

"I—." Kate's words lodged in her throat.

She'd gone to live with several different relatives since eighth grade. Different schools, different states, but the past always caught up with her, branding her forever with the most terrible night of her life.

She'd fled from the prom. Deanna had run after her a few minutes later—but only after furiously berating Wendy for her careless words.

Deanna reached across the plates of macaroni and took Kate's hand. "Jared isn't like those kids in high school. We're all older now. That's just history."

"I'd like to believe it."

"Then do. You've barely dated the past four years. It's time to give someone a chance." Deanna waggled her eyebrows à la Groucho Marx. "Especially him. Like, he's totally awesome. And," she added with a grin, "maybe he has an equally rad brother."

"MAYBE YOU MISUNDERSTOOD and it was, like, next weekend or something." Deanna looked over the top of her pharmacology textbook at the clock on the stove. Almost midnight. "That has to be it."

After washing the dishes, Kate had paced the small apartment for a while, then collapsed on the couch with her homework. "Or he had second thoughts. It's just as well."

"You could call him. Maybe he forgot."

"Even if I wanted to, I lost his number. Not that I'd actually do it."

"You are the most stubborn person I ever met." Deanna flipped to another page in her book and fell silent for a few minutes before looking up again. "By the way, there was a weird guy outside this morning—after you left. He pulled his car to a stop in front of the apartment building and asked Leesa and me a lot of questions."

"He was hitting on you, I bet."

"Yuck. I hope not—he had to be fifty or more. Sorta bald. Business suit."

"You shouldn't talk to strangers, Dee," Kate intoned, mimicking Deanna's mother. "I heard your mom say that *lots* of times."

"Hey, Leesa and I could run faster'n he could, believe me, 'cause he was pretty hefty. He said he was doing a survey of the building and had randomly picked three of the apartments."

"Ours?" Kate made a face. "Did you tell him about the ants? The mold in the bathroom?"

"He mostly asked friendly questions about us.

Where we were from, why we'd moved here, our majors and so on. Oh, and how happy we are with the place, of course. He was really disappointed that he missed talking to you, too."

Kate felt a flash of suspicion. "You didn't tell him anything personal."

Deanna rolled her eyes. "Of course not."

"How do you know that he was who he said he was? Did you call the apartment manager?"

"Leesa and I aren't exactly stupid, thanks very much." Deanna threw her hands up in defeat. "You are *way* too paranoid, but if it makes you feel better, *you* can call."

Mollified, Kate sank back against the cushions and managed a contrite smile. "Sorry. Guess I'm just a little edgy…since Prince Charming didn't show up, and all. Which is just as well, really, because that saves me from any awkward situations later on."

"Like, when you refuse to go out with him again? You oughta be pretty good at shutting guys down by now."

She shrugged, but Deanna wasn't even close. Kate was looking ahead to the situations that might occur if she dared follow her heart and got as far as meeting his family.

She could only imagine what the Matherses

would think if they looked too deeply into her family's past.

The specter of tabloid frenzy would have them barricading their doors.

"YOU'RE SURE it's the same girl?" Sylvia Mathers leaned closer to the entryway mirror and touched the corner of her mouth with a long fingernail, correcting a miniscule smudge of lipstick. "Absolutely sure?"

"Definitely."

Dexter shoved his hands in his pockets, which was infinitely better than watching him fidget with his watch, his wedding band and the cuffs of his suit jacket. And once again, Sylvia second-guessed her decision to send her stuffy brother on such an important mission.

"You talked to this girl? The one Jared told me about on the phone this morning?" She suppressed a shudder. "The one he thinks is his dream girl?"

He twitched, averted his gaze. "Not Kate. She wasn't there. But her roommates were talkative enough. Then I drove clear up to Charlesburg—four hours away—and asked around about her family. As always, you were right. They spell trouble with a capital *T*. Have you told Jared that you were checking up on her background?"

"You know how he is—always leaping to the defense of the downtrodden and misunderstood." Sylvia snorted. "So I simply reminded him of his current and future duty to this family. I also reminded him of his 'long-standing' commitment tonight."

"The children's hospital gala?"

"I told him that he'd promised to be my escort. He brought me home just a few minutes ago. Nice affair, actually. Big crowd, successful benefit." She reined in a tired sigh. "See and be seen, as they say."

"Is it worth it, Syl?" Dexter's voice held a note of reproach. "Maybe your kids don't care about all of this."

"My children are my *life*. And I'm going to see that they take their rightful places in society."

"Well…maybe they want something different for themselves. Maybe they don't care about all the status and money and power."

"Don't care?" Sylvia lifted her chin. "They're too young to understand their father's legacy right now, but they'll thank me in the future. You can bet on it."

"You should be thinking about who you want all this for—you, or them." Dexter regarded her for a long moment, then his shoulders slumped and he turned to the door. "Because I think you're going to drive them away, and then you'll have nothing. Nothing at all."

She clenched her fingers on the back of a chair until her arthritis ached and her knuckles were white, still staring at the door long after Dexter was gone. He had no clue. No clue at all about how hard things were right now.

Which meant, she supposed, that she'd been a success. Smoke and mirrors—her life now amounted to that and nothing more, because Ellsworth had died so young.

A stock market plunge in the eighties had decimated their investments, and he'd been foolish—too focused on his constituents to pay proper attention to his family's financial security.

One avaricious, sleazy little constituent in particular extracted quite a cozy nest egg for herself in exchange for her silence after the senator died in her arms on the dance floor of some tacky bar.

He'd been careless about other matters as well—like maintaining adequate life insurance—and left his family in luxurious housing Sylvia could scarcely afford, with debts beyond anything left in the bank.

So now she worked long hours on full commission in an upscale dress shop, on the pretext that she was simply bored and needed something beyond her volunteer activities to fill her time. She found creative ways to keep up a good front—

buying designer garments and accessories that had been returned to the shop soiled or damaged, and then discounted. Or skillfully refurbishing the classic pieces she already owned.

But above all, she had a plan—a perfect plan—to ensure that the future would be far, far better.

And her children were the ones who could make that happen.

CHAPTER SIX

Present Day

KATE RUBBED HER ARMS, trying to stir some warmth into her cold flesh. Was it twenty degrees in here? Thirty?

At ten o'clock the hallway lights had dimmed, leaving just the harsh glare of ceiling lights in the empty hospital waiting room and the glow of the red exit signs at either end of the hallway she'd been pacing for the last two hours.

Bright light taunted her from behind the double doors marked Staff Only. More than once she'd stopped at those doors to rest her forehead against the frosted windows, willing someone to come out.

Desperately needing to hear good news.

The last announcements hadn't been promising. Blood loss. Concern about reducing the pressure in Jared's brain before permanent damage occurred. From the nurse's grim expression, things were going worse than expected, and there wasn't a single thing Kate could do to help except pray.

She'd certainly kept the line to God open the entire evening—praying Jared would survive, praying that he wouldn't have permanent damage. Praying that Casey and Sylvia would arrive in time for goodbyes if he was beyond hope, though that thought renewed her silent tears every time.

I wish I could go back...do things right. Take back things I've said... I'd be a better wife. A better mom.

The silence of the hospital mocked her as she hesitated at the doors once again, then resumed her pacing.

At the sudden ring of her cell phone she nearly jumped out of her skin, then fumbled to pull it from her jacket pocket. Her heart raced as she squinted at the name on the screen.

"Tom?"

"How are you holding up, Kate?" Jared's law partner's voice was warm and sympathetic, but she could hear a note of hesitance, too.

"All right, I guess. No—" She shoved a hand through her hair. "It's awful, waiting to hear. Casey won't arrive till sometime tomorrow, and Sylvia's on her way."

"But no news is good news, right? He must be holding up in surgery or they would've come out to tell you by now. I'm just so sorry I can't be there with you."

"I wouldn't expect you to be. H-how's Neta?"

"She's doing okay." The single word held a weary acceptance that spoke of all the trials they'd been through with his wife Neta's recurring cancer and coping with their three young children. "I hate to keep you on the phone, but thought you should know that a deputy came out to see me tonight. He left just a few minutes ago."

"About the accident?"

"And about the deceased. We talked at the house, then drove to the office and looked over the planner that Jared keeps on his desk. We couldn't find anything about an appointment this afternoon. There weren't any messages on his office phone, either, and his cell was destroyed in the fire."

Icy fingers clenched Kate's stomach, sending a queasy feeling up her throat. "You have no idea who that woman could have been?"

"None." After a long pause, Tom added, "But there's a lot I don't know about what Jared is handling now."

"Me, too. I know the free clinic is a wonderful concept. There's such need in this county, and it's great that he wants to help. But, well…"

"We've gotten a few anonymous, threatening calls here at the office, and I know you've had some, too." Tom cleared his throat. "I think he's taking on some difficult adversaries."

"That's what I'm afraid of." She shuddered, thinking about the hours she spent on near-deserted roads, going out on farm calls alone. The relative isolation of her own clinic and the house... and the fact that Jared was alone in that free legal clinic into the wee hours of the night.

"The sheriff said he was going over there in the morning to check the appointment book."

Kate swallowed hard. "That woman was probably just a client."

"Of course—of course she was, Kate. Maybe she was a spousal abuse case who walked in off the street and needed a ride to the women's shelter."

But the likelihood of that, with the accident so far south of town, was slim, and they both knew it.

Tom and Jared had been partners since graduation from law school, and he knew about the marriage problems Jared and Kate had been through. His reassurances were those of an old, close friend, but she could hear the overly positive note in his voice.

"The thing now is to just get through this surgery and the recovery," he added gently. "Right?"

"Absolutely. Everything else can be resolved later." Kate sent up another brief prayer, begging for that to be possible. "I—I'll call you whenever I hear anything more."

"Day or night, honey. Neta and I will be by the phone."

Kate snapped her phone shut and dropped it in her pocket. A wave of loneliness and sorrow threatened to buckle her knees, and she sank into a nearby chair, wishing someone would walk through the surgical suite doors *right now* and make the world settle back onto its axis and—

She blinked at the gaunt apparition sitting stiffly in the farthest corner of the waiting room. "*Sylvia.* I didn't hear you come in."

Sylvia sniffed. "I'm sure you didn't."

Though the woman had clearly taken the farthest possible seat on purpose, Kate moved across the room to sit opposite her, scooted a chair closer and reached out to take Sylvia's cold, bony hands between her own.

The woman had always been New-York-model thin, but as she aged, it hadn't served her well. Her skin held a yellowed, waxy pallor and the dark circles under her eyes emphasized her deeply lined face. "You must be absolutely exhausted."

"There was no question, of course. I had to get

here. The nurse in the E.R. said she'd notify surgery that I'd arrived and send someone out with a report. Have you seen anyone?"

"Not for more than an hour. But the last report…" Kate hesitated over just how much to say. "Well, it wasn't very promising. Jared is strong and healthy, and he's a fighter. But his injuries are serious."

Sylvia pulled her hands away and lifted her chin. "He'll make it. The Matherses don't give in."

"I'm praying that's true," Kate said gently. Twenty years of marriage to Jared had never brought companionship, not even acceptance, from his mother, and Kate didn't expect it now. But she knew the stony expression in the woman's eyes hid a great deal of pain that Sylvia had never shared. "He has a lot of people to live for—people who love him. I have to think that it will make a difference."

"Love?" Sylvia's voice sounded like the crack of a whip in the tomblike silence of the hospital. "Don't crow too loudly, my dear. If he loved you so very much, why would he have been driven into the arms of someone else?"

Kate jerked back in her chair, stunned.

"I heard your conversation when I walked in. You might've snared him all those years ago, but it was wrong then, and it's still wrong." Stress and exhaustion and years of simmering dislike seemed to take hold of her, and Sylvia leaned forward, her hands clamped on the arms of her chair and her voice rising. "My son wouldn't be on that surgery table if not for you."

Her thinking was beyond illogical, but there was no point in arguing. Kate silently withdrew to another seat several chairs away.

"You know it's true," Sylvia added in a low, vicious tone. "All the hopes and dreams he had, his bright future, were lost when he was too young to even realize what he was giving up."

The kernel of truth in her words helped Kate bite her tongue when she wanted to refute every word, but none of this was new. Critical, cold and relentless, Sylvia had found endless ways to drive home subtle barbs over the years about their marriage. Her advancing age had only sharpened her tongue…but she'd always been crafty enough to guard what she said within her son's hearing.

At the sound of rattling wheels—gurney wheels?—Kate shot to her feet, a hand over her heart.

A cleaning woman wearily trudged down the hall, pushing a cart of supplies.

Five endless minutes later, the double doors to

surgery swung open, bathing the hall in blinding light. The surgeon stepped forward, his face haggard beneath his five o'clock shadow, the surgical mask hanging in front of his neck.

Kate's heart skipped a beat, stumbled, then started pounding as her anxiety grew. He seemed to be walking toward her in ultraslow motion, while she couldn't will herself to move a single step toward the news that might change her life forever.

Then time stopped as numbness swept through her. "Is he… Is he…"

The words couldn't get past the lump in her throat.

Dr. Jacobs reached out to take her hand. "Honestly, I had my doubts, but he's still with us. He coded several times. We had trouble bringing him back the last time. The next twenty-four hours are going to be critical."

She swallowed hard, dimly aware that Sylvia had come to stand next to her, her back ramrod straight in preparation for the worst possible news.

"Critical." Sylvia knotted her fists at her sides. "Clarify that, please."

"You are…"

"His mother, naturally. Sylvia Mathers."

Sympathy warmed Jacobs's eyes. "Your son is a lucky man. In cases like this we need rapid assessment and immediate evacuation to an appropriate medical facility—within an hour or less. He was here within that golden hour, and fortunately, surgeons experienced with his types of injuries were available."

"Thank God for that," Kate whispered.

"With hematomas or depressed skull fractures, the immediate risk is dangerously elevated intracranial pressure and brain damage. We've placed a temporary catheter to help drain excess fluids, and so we can closely monitor him for rising pressure."

"And if that happens?"

"We've already started IV Lasix, but we've got other options… We'll just have to see how he does. We'll also be monitoring him for blood clots. I promise you," Jacobs said with a ghost of a smile, "that he will have the best of care."

Sylvia frowned. "When can I see my son?"

The doctor glanced at the clock on the wall. "He's in recovery now, then he'll be transported to the ICU. Maybe you two can go home and get some rest, and come back in a few hours? You'll only be able to sit with him for a few minutes every hour, anyway."

Anxiety rippled through Kate at the thought of leaving the hospital—leaving Jared here without family—even for an hour. She turned to Sylvia.

"I'll stay, if you'd like to go out to the house. I can give you the keys."

"I called for hotel reservations on my way here."

"But—"

"I think it would be best, don't you?" The frosty tone in her voice gave no room for discussion. "We'll all be more comfortable."

Dr. Jacobs looked between them and cleared his throat. "If you'll excuse me, ladies, I need to check in on Jared and write my surgical report. You can ask the nurses to contact me if you have any questions."

As soon as he was gone, Kate tried again. "Are you sure you want to be alone? Casey will be home tomorrow, and we have two empty bedrooms. It would be nice for you two to have some time together."

Sylvia turned to gather her purse and a light jacket she'd draped across the back of a chair. "Perhaps *you'll* have some time to spare. But I assure you, this hospital is where I plan to spend my time. I'm going to settle in at the hotel, and I'll be back in an hour."

Kate listened to the sharp staccato click of her high heels fading down the hall, the oppressive weight of two difficult decades descending upon her. As she slowly made her way to the ICU in the east wing, Kate tried to focus on positive thoughts. Tried to sympathize with an old, bitter woman still dwelling in the past and too caught up in her anger to set aside her differences with her son's wife, even in the face of Jared's critical injuries.

But Sylvia had rejected every opportunity for opening herself up to a loving relationship with her son's family. She'd suffered for it, Kate was sure…and so had Kate and Casey and Jared. *Feel sorry for her,* Kate muttered to herself as she waited for the elevator. *She must be terribly lonely.*

But sympathy was hard to gather.

Her mother-in-law's parting barb had hit the mark with perfect accuracy as always, conjuring up the memories of too many cutting remarks to count…

And the one Kate had never been able to forgive.

CHAPTER SEVEN

The Past

STUDYING LIPID METABOLISM and neuro-spinal pathways was an excellent antidote to any propensity to dwell on the mysterious Jared Mathers, who had seemed so interested and then managed to drop off the earth.

Which was just as well.

Kate flicked a glance at her watch and drew in a sharp breath. Between her temporary part-time job in a bovine mastitis research lab, a tight schedule of classes and long labs, there wasn't enough time. There was never enough—and nothing mattered more than acing her exams and staying near the top of her class.

Her scholarships and plans to go on to surgical residency depended on it.

Sometime, maybe in five years, she'd be able to slow down and try for some semblance of a social life. Until then—

"Hi, there."

Startled, she looked up and saw Jared standing at the other side of the table. A thick dusting of early-November snow clung to the deep waves in his hair and to the shoulders of his navy ski jacket.

"I…wondered if you might have time for a cup of coffee somewhere." A self-conscious smile tipped one corner of his mouth. "I know it's been a while…"

He had the most mesmerizing eyes. Smoky gray and sensual, yet with a glint of humor that captivated her every time. She averted her gaze. "I can't."

"Maybe another time?"

The temptation before her was like facing a display of her favorite caramels and milk chocolates in a candy store window—an all-too-enticing opportunity that could lead to her downfall. "Honestly, I am so swamped with classes and homework right now that I barely have time to sleep."

He pulled out a chair and settled into it, folding his arms on the table. "I want to apologize for not showing up a few weeks ago. I'd forgotten about a family commitment, and there was no way I could back out of it. I tried calling you, but the line was busy every time."

"I was home." Kate shrugged. "But I don't remember—maybe Leesa's new cat was playing with the phone again and knocked it off the hook."

Could that have been the case? Probably not. There was no point in being difficult, but that didn't mean she was going to be available just because he now had some time on his hands. And she couldn't afford to stop cramming for her test, either.

He reached into his jacket pocket, pulled out a small brown paper sack and pushed it across the table toward her. His smile turned sheepish. "I saw this at my favorite corner store a few weeks ago while I was doing time there. It isn't much, but it made me think of you."

"So you did go back there."

He lifted a shoulder. "Had to."

She hesitated, then reached into the bag and pulled out an object wrapped in tissue paper. Inside, she found a glass figurine of a golden retriever. "It's darling. But—"

"It's just something small. Not a big deal. And in case you're wondering," he added with a tip of his head, "it isn't a bribe to try to make amends."

The retriever was almost a perfect rendition of her beloved Emma, who'd died last year, Kate's dearest friend in the world. A coincidence? She felt her eyes burn.

Jared seemed to read her thoughts. "I saw the photo of you and your dog on your desk, the night we shared that pizza."

"Thank you," she breathed, cradling the dog in her hands. "You don't know how much this means to me."

He glanced at her stack of textbooks and pushed away from the table. "I guess I'd better be going, so I can hit the books, too. See you around."

He'd followed through and kept his word to a store clerk. He'd been thoughtful enough to see a little figurine and think of her. And he'd apparently kept a family commitment above a casual social commitment of his own…which she could understand. "Wait—"

At the nearby tables, students looked up and frowned at her, but she didn't care. With the vet school on the Saint Paul campus and the law school over on the Minneapolis campus, maybe she'd never even see him again.

She caught up with him at the door to the stairway. "I…just wanted to thank you for thinking of me. And for coming all the way over here."

"No problem." He zipped up his jacket. "Good seeing you again."

There was an invisible barrier between them now, and she didn't know what to say. "I—I'll be free after my exams tomorrow. In the evening…"

He shrugged. "I have to be with my study group. Tax law."

"Maybe we can study together some other time."

"Maybe." He pulled open the door. "Look, I know you aren't all that interested, but maybe I'll give you a call sometime. Deal?"

She nodded, feeling the chasm widen between them. Wishing she were like Deanna and Leesa, who always seemed to have guys following them like imprinted ducklings, and who could draw new recruits with a single teasing glance. "Deal."

He disappeared down the steps, but even after he was gone she lingered at the door.

He'd touched her in some indefinable way, and now she found herself drawn even deeper into his spell. Her entire life had been one of daring to go beyond expectations. Facing challenges. Taking risks. Except when it came to her heart.

Call me, she whispered to herself as she turned back to the responsibilities that lay strewn across the library table. *Please.*

She'd barely settled down to study when the stairway door squealed open and Jared came back in and strode across the room with a determined set to his jaw and a twinkle in his eye.

He grabbed her jacket from the back of her chair. Took her hand. "Come with me now. Just five minutes."

Dazed and feeling unaccountably giddy, she

let him lead her down the stairs, across the lobby and out into the cold night air, where immense snowflakes swirled on the chilly breeze like lacy doilies beneath the security lights. Already, the tall pines were dressed in heavy, sparkling mantles of white, and the snow on the sidewalks was ankle deep.

"It's too beautiful not to share," he said, drawing her into the warmth of his strong embrace. "Coming out here made me realize that you're the only one I'd like to share this with. I'm not a quitter, Kate."

He looked down at her for a long, heart-stopping moment, his face shadowed by the lights overhead. "And I'm not walking away from something that's so right."

A thrill of awareness rushed through her when he kissed her. She melted against him, feeling as if she'd always been part of him, as if she'd known him from the beginning of time. And when he pulled back, she impulsively wrapped her arms around his neck and drew him to her again.

"I think," he said after he'd caught his breath, "that we'd be crazy not to see each other again."

She leaned her forehead against the solid wall of his chest. "Agreed."

"Tomorrow?"

"I—I still do have to study…and need to write a paper."

"Good. We'll meet here then, at the library. Maybe grab a hamburger or something before?"

She thought of the change in her purse that had to stretch until Saturday. "Um…my place, maybe? All I've got is mac 'n' cheese or hot dogs, but it's cheap and paid for."

"Great." He kissed the tip of her nose and released her. "Tomorrow, then."

She watched him jog toward the campus bus stop, her heart overflowing.

It wouldn't last. These things never did…not when he learned about her family. Especially not if he happened to meet her mom.

But for a little while, she was going to enjoy her time with this perfect, unattainable stranger.

And what could be wrong with that?

NOVEMBER PASSED in a whirl of study dates. Meeting over coffee or pizza or yet another box of generic macaroni with neon orange cheese. Just being with Jared warmed her clear down to her toes, and hearing his voice on the phone sent shivers skittering down her spine.

Heavy snow had come hard, fast and early, turning the side streets near the university into rutted pioneer trails that were nearly impassable in her ancient pickup, even with sandbags stacked over the rear axles, and kept the campus buses limited to only the major streets more often than not.

Now, with Thanksgiving break just a day away, Kate looked out the kitchen window of her apartment at the bleak snowscape and shivered as yet another blast of icy air whistled through the window frame. Already, the sky was darkening, and with another four inches starting to fall, the street outside was nearly deserted.

She turned back to Jared. "I appreciate the invitation to have Thanksgiving dinner with your family. Honestly, I do. But I need to stay here. I've got that parasitology paper due, and an exam on equine musculature Monday."

"It's not that far, and we'd come back in the evening. Wayzata's an hour, tops. There won't be any rush hour traffic on a holiday, and even with the snow—"

"I just can't." The weight on her heart made it seem harder to breathe. Why hadn't she fessed up already? Told him the truth? Waiting had only made the issue loom larger, compounding her guilt and her sense of shame.

It would look all the worse when she finally got up her nerve to tell him.

He leaned back in his chair, studying her, his expression losing its warmth. "I don't get it."

She'd been falling deeper and deeper in love. An impossible relationship, because once she was honest with him, it would all be over. "I…haven't exactly told you everything. About my family."

"Easy guess. Single mom. Not exactly wealthy, right? A pretty tough childhood?" He raised his hands, palm up, his voice tinged with reproach. "None of that matters. I'm kind of disappointed that you think I'm that shallow."

"But—"

He rocked forward in his chair, slanted a glance at the darkening twilight and grabbed his backpack from the floor as he rose. "Look, I'll pick you up tomorrow. Say, eleven o'clock. We can go out to my mom's for dinner, and I'll have you back here by seven." He pulled on his heavy jacket, swung his backpack over one shoulder and gave her a one-armed hug and a kiss. "It won't seem like a holiday if you can't be with me."

She stood in the open doorway of the apartment and waved to him when he reached the stairway at the end of the hall.

Chicken, she muttered to herself. *You are so gutless. You could have told him.*

Still, she now had one more day. A chance to see

his home and to meet his mother and younger sister. A chance to make some more memories. A chance to spend the whole day with him. And how perfect was that? She wanted to make every minute count.

THE TWIN CITIES were beautiful year-round to a girl from the far northwestern plains of Minnesota near the Dakotas.

At every turn, lakes were tucked like jewels in unexpected places, and during the warmer weather, the endless parks and tree-shaded streets beckoned to hikers and dog-walkers and families pushing strollers.

Now, as she sat beside Jared on their way out to Wayzata, the snow-frosted pines reminded Kate of her grandmother's snow globe, and the city lakes abounded with skating rinks and children dressed in bright colors skimming across the ice.

But when they reached Wayzata and started to drive around the lake, her joy faded into a serious case of nerves.

Tidy suburban homes had long since given way to attractive lakeshore properties, followed by one gated estate after another.

Stone walls and dense stands of pine hid most of the homes, but here and there she glimpsed multiple chimneys signifying a palatial house, or caught a peek of a stone dwelling that could've been a British castle for all of its many turrets and massive scale.

"Tell me that we've got a long way to go to your mother's home," Kate whispered, staring at an ostentatious set of iron gates and pillars marking the driveway of yet another expensive property.

Jared glanced at her as he hit a remote button on his visor that made the gates swing open, then flipped on the turn signal.

"Here?" She swallowed hard. "You live *here?*"

He shrugged. "My family does. Nervous?"

"Um…a little."

"Don't be. It's just a house." He turned into a long lane flanked with white fencing that wound up a hill, past stands of pine and a forest of winter-bare oaks. At the top of the hill, the lane opened into a wide, circular drive that arced under the portico of a two-story redbrick home easily the size of her small-town high school.

Her mouth dropped open and she quickly snapped it shut, hoping he hadn't noticed. "You…grew up here?" she managed to ask.

"From tenth grade on." He lifted a shoulder. "My father inherited it from my grandmother."

"I-it's beautiful." She stepped out of his car and turned around to find that the hill offered an impressive view of Lake Minnetonka. "You must love this place."

"It's nice, I guess, but it's expensive for my mother to maintain. You wouldn't believe how the real estate taxes, care of the grounds and heating bills add up."

She managed a polite nod, well aware that he was diplomatically minimizing the astounding family wealth that had to be behind a home like this, just to make her more comfortable. Jared didn't flaunt his family's money—he drove an older Mustang and mostly dressed like any other college guy.

But now she knew his Rolex was real, and if they'd just landed on Mars, she couldn't have felt more out of place than she did arriving at his home.

"Come on, let's go inside," he said, taking her hand when she lingered by the car. "It's cold out here, and I promise you that my mom doesn't bite."

"I'm sure she's lovely." Kate followed him up the broad front steps to the double doors, each set with mullioned windows. "Will this just be… um…the immediate family?"

"Just my sister, mom and us. My uncle Dexter and his family are with his wife's relatives in Chicago. You can call my mother by her first name, by the way. Sylvia."

Inside, the entry gave way to a two-story reception area flanked by a sweeping, curved staircase leading to the second floor. Jared took her jacket and his and tossed them on a velvet fainting couch set in front of the windows.

Imagining butlers and cooks scurrying around behind the scenes, Kate expected to see Mrs. Mathers glide down the staircase in a formal gown, but Jared motioned for Kate to follow, leading the way to the kitchen, where a slender, elegant woman stood at a butcher-block island, eyeing a golden turkey with a measure of distaste.

She looked up and smiled at Jared, offering her cheek for a quick kiss, gave Kate a dismissive glance, then continued to study the offending bird. "I'm not sure it's big enough. Do you think so, dear?"

"It looks fantastic. This is Kate, by the way."

Kate moved forward, extending her hand. "It's so nice to meet you."

Sylvia nodded politely without accepting the handshake, her face expressionless. "I'll make sure we have *lots* of time to talk a little later."

"When can we eat?" Jared peered around her to an open doorway. "Is the table set? Can we help?"

His mother's light laugh was silvery, as elegant as she was in her slim black dress and pearls. "I had dinner delivered just minutes ago, and everything else is on the sideboard. If you'll carry in this platter and help me carve, we can start."

"Where's Julia?"

"Your sister *insisted* on going with your Uncle Dex, so she could spend the weekend with her cousins. So I'm afraid it's just the three of us."

Outside, the wind picked up, slamming crystalline snow against the windows. Inside, Kate felt a similar chill. Was it her imagination…or had Jared's mother just taken an instant dislike to her?

"THIS WAS A WONDERFUL MEAL," Jared said as he folded his napkin and placed it next to his plate. "The caterers did a terrific job."

"As always," Sylvia murmured. She tipped her head at Kate. "I'm sure your family has a big get-together and everyone helps out with the cooking, but it's just three of us for holidays. I've never been particularly gifted in the kitchen, at any rate. So I have everything catered."

"That makes perfect sense," Kate murmured.

Throughout the meal, Sylvia had spoken to her only twice, and that had been to request the salt or pepper. Still, the woman had emanated a strange sense of satisfaction when Kate surreptitiously watched Jared for cues on the proper forks and spoons to pick up for each course.

Apparently oblivious to the uncomfortable undercurrents in the room, Jared had remained his usual congenial self, talking to both of them, regaling them with stories about some of his more challenging moments in law school. If he noticed his mother's frosty behavior, he gave no sign.

Sylvia looked over her wineglass at her son. "If you're done, darling, could you possibly bring in some firewood? We can lay a fire in the living room and have our dessert there."

Kate rose to gather the plates when Jared left the table, but Sylvia motioned her to sit back with a dismissive flick of her hand. "We'll get these things later. I'd rather have a chance to talk."

A premonition wrapped icy tentacles around Kate's stomach. "It was a lovely dinner. Thanks so much for the invitation, Mrs. Mathers."

"I'm afraid it wasn't my idea. It was Jared's, of course, but perhaps it's just as well." Sylvia bared her teeth in a wintry smile. "You see, my dear, you seem to have a very troubling past, and I want you out of his life. So now I'm just wondering… How much do you want him to know?"

CHAPTER EIGHT

KATE JERKED HER GAZE to the windows, wishing she could see past the reflections to the darkness outside.

"It will be a while before Jared comes back," Sylvia said mildly. "The storage building is at the far end of the backyard. There's plenty of time for us to work through these little details."

"I—I don't know what you mean." Kate's heart pounded as if it were trying to break free of her chest.

"Perhaps you'd like to take Jared to Charlesburg to meet your mother? Or to catch up on some of the local gossip?" Sylvia pursed her lips. "I'm sure Francine Becker is still quite a hot topic these days. She *is* your mother, right?"

"Yes," Kate whispered, closing her eyes.

"I'm sorry—I didn't quite hear you."

"*Yes.* Yes, she is."

Sylvia shook her head sadly. "It must have been quite awkward for her, killing your father like that. Murder is such an ugly word."

"It was an accident." Kate gripped the back of a chair with both hands. "He came into the kitchen. They were arguing…and he stumbled into the knife she held in her hand. *Accidentally.*"

"A pity that the judge and jury didn't think so, dear. But perhaps you don't remember all the facts quite right. You were what—in third grade? And the stress of testifying surely must have been something you wanted to forget."

"It's something I think about every day."

"Then you must understand my concerns."

Kate looked down at her white knuckles. Even now that she was an adult, the shame and fear and panic sometimes came rushing back in vivid images, leaving her in a cold sweat and breathing hard. "I lost my dad, and then I lost my mom, too, for the six long years she was incarcerated. *Wrongly* incarcerated."

Sylvia flipped a hand dismissively. "Wrongly or not, I'm afraid you have quite a past…and I'm very afraid of what that could do to Jared's future if you two ever, well…"

"We're barely *dating!*"

"But things can happen." She made a moue of distaste. "A girl is careless—perhaps even on purpose. There's a necessary marriage, and then there you have it. An alliance that could destroy Jared's future."

Until now Kate had felt self-conscious and out of place in this grand home. But she felt a flare of outraged anger at the woman's assumptions. "I'm hardly wanting to trap your son, Mrs. Mathers. I'm in vet school, and I have career goals, too. Marriage and parenthood—in whatever order they occur—have no place in my plans for the next *decade*."

"Things happen all the same."

"Not with me." Kate glanced again at the darkened windows, wishing she could leave this place without making a scene.

Sylvia toyed with her wineglass, took a sip and studied the sparkling cut of the crystal. "Let me put this another way. What do you see, when you look around this house?"

Caught off guard, Kate darted a quick glance at the towering wall of windows that probably faced a manicured back lawn. The heavy antique dining-room table that could easily seat twenty. A massive, gilt-framed painting of an Edwardian lady, undoubtedly an original.

"I…guess I see an elegant home," she ventured. "You have beautiful taste."

"What you see, my dear, is a house of cards." Sylvia waved a hand toward the glass-fronted hutch, where backlight displayed the fine crystal, then at the glittering chandelier. "This place will belong to Jared and Julia someday. It's a home for entertaining, for impressing people who must be impressed. My late husband and I hosted many a political fundraiser here. Dinners and festive parties that helped him move forward with his career."

She stood and paced the room, then stopped by Kate's chair. "You are a lovely girl. I can see why Jared is attracted to you. But can you imagine him graduating law, then trying to follow his father's footsteps with a wife from such a…difficult background?"

"I have no plans—"

"The tabloids would have a field day, believe me. These days they're like ravenous sharks. His chances for the prestigious law firms, the most influential positions, might be seriously damaged." Sylvia slid into the chair next to Kate and took her hand. "I've held on to this place since Ellsworth died because of my children. There's no way they'd be able to hang on to it if Jared's career wasn't a shining success. Do you love him?"

Kate felt heat rise up her neck and into her cheeks. "No…well…we haven't really been together that long, and…"

"If you care at all about him, step away. Don't let things go any further."

"But I'm not like my parents."

"Look, I know about the child abuse charges against your father, and that he was an alcoholic. Your mom, too. Is that why she failed to protect your brother?" Sylvia's voice hardened. "Do you want all of that history splashed across the magazines? Isn't Kyle a first grade teacher now? What would that humiliation do to his new career? And to Jared's political future, if he were to marry into such a family? If he runs for the senate, as his father did, your life will be an open book."

Kate felt her stomach twist. Kyle had suffered, protecting her from their father. How could she fail to protect him now, in return?

Apparently satisfied, Sylvia sat back in her chair. "I won't make a scene over this, as long as you stay away from my son. He never even needs to know we had this talk."

Her stomach tightened even more, and all Kate could do was stare silently back at Sylvia in disbelief.

"Honestly," Sylvia continued, "the past will probably never come back to haunt any of you if you're not in the limelight. Please, I beg you— don't ruin Jared's life."

"YOU'RE AWFULLY QUIET," Jared said reaching for Kate's hand as they came out of a small neighborhood movie theater near the campus. "Didn't you like the movie?"

"Loved it. Daniel Day-Lewis is *amazing*. The woman who played his mom, too." Kate breathed easier, thankful for an innocuous topic. "*My Left Foot* ought to earn them some major awards."

Two weeks after Thanksgiving, and she still hadn't been able to walk away from him, though Sylvia's threat was never far from her thoughts. The knowledge that she was a potential liability for Jared was even more unsettling.

If she told him why she was leaving, she knew he'd stick by her no matter what. But if she selfishly remained silent and stayed, how could she hurt the man she'd come to love?

"I've been thinking," she said slowly.

"Sounds like trouble," he teased, giving her hand an extra squeeze.

This was so difficult. "You and I are both incredibly busy. Maybe we should just back off for a while."

"Bad idea." He playfully bumped his upper arm against her shoulder. "Bad, bad, bad."

"I mean it." She took a deep breath. "I can't afford to think about anything else except school. I've been distracted these past couple months, and if I don't keep my GPA up, it could ruin everything. Just look at how much time we spend going between the two campuses to see each other."

"You're kidding, right?" He slowed to a stop, his gaze riveted on hers. "This is just a joke."

"No. It's not." She had to look away, because otherwise she would cave in.

"Sorry, I don't buy it. Look, if you're feeling pressured right now, we can just talk on the phone, and you can live at that library of yours. A whole month, if that's what it takes."

"It's bigger than that, Jared." He fell silent, and she knew how much she was hurting him. "This next year or two are going to be overwhelming for me. I hear all of the upper level students talking about it. I just need my space."

"It doesn't have to be this way. I don't want to lose you, Kate."

"Ending this relationship is the best thing you could do for the both of us. Don't you see that? Look at where you come from. What your plans are. Do you have any idea how badly things could work out? We need to end this now."

He rocked back on his heels and swore under his breath. "It's about that house. My so-called 'family heritage.'"

"And your future," she blurted out, desperate to

make him see the truth. If he took her into his arms, she would never have the strength to walk away.

"My future," he repeated flatly.

"Your dad was an influential senator. You can be one, too, if you want. But if you're saddled with me, what chances would you have? Can you see the headlines?"

"What would they be, Kate?" he asked evenly, his eyes growing colder. "Got any secrets you need to share?"

"More dirty laundry than you can even imagine." She took a few steps away and sank onto a bus stop bench. "But the more I think about it, the more I realize that I really don't want to share the kind of future you'll have, anyway."

"Even if I end up as some lowly small-town lawyer, instead of a senatorial hotshot?" He stood in front of her and managed a faint smile that didn't begin to reach his eyes. "In case you're at all curious, I've never thought about politics. Not even once."

"I guess I'm just saying that we should stop seeing each other. It's been nice, but I don't think it was meant to be."

"Nice?" He lingered for a long moment, then slowly shook his head. "You surprise me, Kate. I never thought we'd end up like this."

Guilt made it impossible for her to answer, though the pain in his voice tore at her heart.

"My father is gone, along with his money. The unspoken assumption was that I'd do my duty and marry well to rescue the family fortunes." Jared gave a short, cynical laugh. "I would have given up anything to be with you. *Anything.* But I guess we're all in luck, because love won't be standing in the way of duty now."

And then he walked away.

DECEMBER DRAGGED on into January, snowfall upon snowfall, then the endless rain and mud of a very wet spring…one exam, paper and difficult lab after another.

Kate's initial excitement over her admission to vet school was now replaced by a quieter sense of accomplishment and the thrill of meeting every challenge head-on…until it came to dealing with the parakeets.

"I had a little trouble yesterday," she admitted to Deanna. "Two of 'em got loose in the room and took forever to catch, and then I had a problem drawing a blood sample. Thanks for coming with me today."

"I owe you, after you helped me review for the bovine dystocia test." Deanna looked across the exam table and grinned. "You've never had birds?"

"I wanted them when I was in grade school. My mom said she was allergic. My dad said they smelled like chickens, and he wouldn't allow them in the house." Kate laughed. "Come to think of it, they gave the same excuses for hedgehogs, guinea pigs and gerbils."

"You poor, deprived baby."

"I had all sorts of reptiles and rodents in cages out in the barn, and the usual cats and dogs, plus the livestock on my uncle's farm. Just never had any experience with birds. And," Kate added with a grin, "I think birds can sense that a mile off."

"Well, we're the only ones here, so it's a good time to practice." Deanna opened the cage door and deftly corralled a hapless bird within her cupped hands. A wild rustling of feathers ensued, and she flinched. "Pecked me, the little bugger."

When the bird calmed, they started working from the lab instruction sheet on the table between them, listening to the creature's rapid heartbeat. Examining it for psittacosis, BPFD and overall health, followed by a blood draw and fecal exam.

"Your turn," Deanna said after replacing the bird in the cage. "Let's see… Try for that green-and-yellow one."

The bird apparently had excellent hearing,

because it promptly flapped and clawed its way to the topmost bar of the cage.

Kate nearly had it, when it scrambled away in a flurry of airborne feathers. She finally snared the struggling bird—only to have it shoot out of her grasp like a wet bar of soap.

"These birds haven't been socialized, so we've got a bigger challenge." Deanna chuckled. "It's a trick, all right. Hold them too tight and they'll keel over dead. Too loose, and they're gone."

When Kate finally managed to capture the bird, she let it rest for a few minutes within her cupped hands before bringing it out. She started going through each step of the exam under Deanna's watchful eye.

But after a few minutes, she realized Deanna had fallen silent, her expression distracted. "What's wrong?"

Deanna bit her lower lip. "Nothing…probably."

"Nothing."

"Well, not anything that should matter. You know, when a person breaks up with someone, they don't mind when they hear some news about them, right?"

"This is confusing."

Deanna shifted her weight, clearly uneasy. "Though I'd guess these things can hurt, even if you aren't supposed to care anymore."

Kate stilled. "Tell me."

"I figured you should maybe hear it first from me, so it won't be a surprise at some really awkward time."

If she hadn't been holding a bird, Kate might have succumbed to the temptation to grab Deanna's shoulders and shake her. *"What?"*

Deanna looked down at the table. "Jared."

A chill gripped Kate's heart as she imagined the terrible things that could've happened. "Is he… Is he all right?"

"I heard he's…um…engaged."

Speechless, Kate stared at her.

"To some really wealthy girl—and they aren't waiting around for a long engagement, either. What a jerk, right? I mean, it's been, what—six months? How shallow is that? He never did deserve you, that's for sure. Not when he could go off like this and…"

Deanna's voice vibrated with loyalty and indignation, but her tirade faded into the distance as Kate processed the news and felt the empty chasm in her chest grow until it pressed against her ribs.

Engaged.

A day hadn't gone by without images of Jared crowding into her mind. Regrets. Memories. Wishful thoughts. Daydreams in which he would appear one day like her white knight, insisting that nothing would ever again keep them apart.

Silly thoughts, because she'd been the one to end their relationship. She'd sacrificed her fanciful romantic dreams to make sure he had every option open to him for his future, and that wasn't something she could undo.

But now, the door was truly closed.

CHAPTER NINE

Present Day

EVEN THE ICU LIGHTING was muted during the wee hours of the morning; the constant soft beeps, clicks and the low hum of various motors added a surreal, futuristic feel to the otherwise eerie hush belying the life-and-death struggle of the two patients lying inside the unit.

Kate watched through the window of the waiting room as a nurse walked to the far end where Jared lay, pulled back the white curtain and hovered over his bed to check his IV lines.

She adjusted his pillow and checked the heavy bandaged dressing on his head, then rejoined the other two nurses who were working at the computers in the central nursing station. Illuminated by the blue glow of their computer screens and the banks of monitors relaying every breath, every heartbeat of their patients, they seemed totally efficient and impersonal, until one of them turned to the others and said something to make them laugh.

It was comforting, seeing human emotion break free amidst the tension of this place. Perhaps it was just that this was a quiet night. Only two patients, with the other four curtained bays empty, prepped and waiting for the next critical care situation.

Who knew when that might happen? A twist of fate—one wrong step—a millisecond of hesitation…

If Jared had left his office a second sooner, would he be here, fighting for his life? Or would he be sleeping soundly at home?

The chaplain arrived, spoke quietly to the nurses and moved to the patient in the bay next to Jared's, communion tray in hand.

Kate had to look away from that intimate moment of faith, the preparation for a final journey home.

The chaplain had already been to see Jared, and it gave her a somber sense of peace, but even now she wanted to defy the rules and stride to his bedside. Urge him to fight for his life…to open his eyes and see how much his family still needed him. *You can't leave us, sweetheart…not now. Not with so many years left.*

But she'd had the last visit, and in thirteen minutes Sylvia would have her own turn to sit with him for those five precious minutes every hour. And Kate would have to wait—she looked at her watch—until 6:05 a.m.

Seventy-eight minutes to pray that no alarms would go off. That the nurses wouldn't need to rush to Jared's side and sound a code blue.

Seventy-eight minutes to hope and pray that he would still be here on earth at the end of them.

Sylvia sat behind her in a leather chair, stiffly erect after all this time. She'd declined the offer of a pillow and blanket, choosing to sit silently by herself, lost in her own thoughts.

Did she ever have any regrets over the things she'd said and done? Her cold rejection of Kate these many years?

Kate turned to offer her a cup of coffee from the fresh pot brewing at the back of the lounge. Sylvia's eyes had finally closed, her head lolling slightly to one side, though she still held her old-fashioned handbag firmly in her lap with both hands.

You need your rest whether you'll admit it or not, Kate thought, with a rush of compassion. *It's been a long, hard night for all of us.*

OLD BONES and hospital chairs were a combination devised by the devil himself.

Sylvia stirred, winced at the pain shooting through her bad hip and forced herself to ignore it.

Mind over matter. Weak people whined and complained and expected people to fawn. She didn't need that. Wouldn't accept it.

Everything was a choice in this life.

A choice to live, a choice to wither and die.

A choice to let anger and bitterness corrode the soul, or to let past wrongs drift away like refuse on a cold, dark sea. She'd been letting it all drift lately…and the sea surrounding her was toxic with it. All the wrongs that had been done to her over the years suffocating her.

She'd held on to her anger and resentment like a lifeline, meting out judgment and punishment with stony silence. She'd felt self-righteous in her solitude.

But now her only son…her estranged only son…lay on a hospital bed, quite possibly dying, and there was no way she could make things right. The weight of her guilt settled around her heart like an iron fist, threatening to crush it.

She sucked in a sharp breath as another pain shot through her and sent dizzying stars spinning through her head. The bum hip, or was it somewhere…higher…?

A wave of cold sweat and nausea rolled through

her and she clenched the arms of the chair, willing it to recede. She had no time for this.

It was her son that mattered now. Only her son.

She would hang on and make sure he didn't give up. She didn't tolerate quitters. She had the strength, the iron will, to make sure he didn't let go. Not like Ellsworth, who'd so easily given up.

She gritted her teeth until her jaw ached, and fixed her eyes on the clock.

Three minutes to go and then she could march to Jared's bedside and *will* him to fight for his life.

He wouldn't dare defy her.

She wasn't weak, not like the woman he'd rebelliously taken for his wife. Sylvia's old anger and disappointment threatened to surface but she held it at bay. Kate meant nothing. It was Jared who mattered now. He needed her.

And this time, she wouldn't fail him.

The Past

SYLVIA ADJUSTED her smart little hat and took another close look at her lipstick in the entryway mirror of her home. There would be many old friends at the country club this afternoon, all there in celebration of Jared's engagement to the youngest Hastings girl.

Sheila was a prime catch, with her boarding

school education and her recent graduation from Northwestern. Her new position as assistant buyer for her father's chain of upscale department stores was icing on the proverbial cake.

What could be better than an alliance such as this?

Smiling at herself in the mirror, Sylvia straightened her pearls, then glanced back into the cavernous front hall and breathed a sigh of pure relief.

The past few years had been a desperate struggle to keep the place going. Taxes and repairs and the abominable groundskeeper who charged far too much had drained her investments, but keeping up the show had been worth every penny.

The Hastings girl hardly would've been impressed by a young man living in a little rambler in the suburbs. And now, with her future guaranteed in her father's company and her substantial trust funds, Jared would be stepping into the world for which he'd been destined, and his ten-year-old sister, Julia, would still have her chance to shine someday.

And Sylvia would no longer need to fear financial ruin. Ellsworth had managed his money poorly, leaving her with far too little, but the children would soon be able to provide for her. She had no doubt about that.

Jared's footsteps sounded on the staircase and she smiled in his direction as he approached.

"Well, dear…are you ready for your big day? This will be—" Her voice failed when she took in his haggard expression, his sweatshirt and faded jeans. "Good heavens. It's time to go. Why aren't you dressed?"

"I can't go through with this, Mother. I tried, but I can't." He dropped into a chair and rested his forearms on his thighs, his head bowed.

Panic rushed through Sylvia with lightning speed. "Don't be silly. You've asked this girl and she accepted. Everyone gets cold feet—it happens all the time. But it's *nothing*."

He lifted his weary eyes to meet hers. "But that's exactly what I feel. Nothing."

"But she's a sweet, smart girl. Educated. Lovely to talk to. Don't get so wrapped up in yourself that you forget just how special she really is." Hearing her own voice rising, Sylvia took a steadying breath. "This is just a silly case of nerves, darling. Go get dressed, and we can be off."

"No, we can't. This was just a bad case of rebound, on both sides. Sheila's longtime boyfriend dumped her. We both just needed a friend."

Sylvia curbed her rising anger. "Kate? You didn't *lose* that little tramp. Nothing so sad and heart-wrenching as that, so don't let her destroy something as special as your chance with Sheila. Kate walked out on you, plain and simple. And do you know why?"

Jared's eyes widened and she could see the realization dawning in his expression. "What did you say to her?"

"Nothing that wasn't the absolute truth. Not that she was very forthcoming about the truth to you, by the way. Did she ever tell you about her background?"

"Of course she did. She said there was 'plenty of dirty laundry in her past.' So what? What family hasn't had some bad turns along the way?"

"She didn't elaborate? Tell you about her alcoholic parents? Or tell you that her mother served *seven years* in prison for murdering her father? What kind of family connection would that be, for heaven's sake? Being mixed up with such rabble would've led to your professional ruin."

"*What,* exactly, did you tell her?" Jared's voice vibrated with anger.

"I told her the truth, sweetheart. That all of this…this pretentious lifestyle of ours—"

"*Yours,* Mother."

Sylvia ignored him. "I told her that this was all just a house of cards. That despite appearances, there's no great wealth here—no opportunity for a golden, pampered future simply by marrying into the family."

Jared launched to his feet, shoving his hair back with both hands as he paced across the floor, then returned. "So you essentially called her a gold digger."

"No, but clearly she was. Didn't she walk out on you a few weeks after she was here and learned the truth? Have you heard from her since?" Sylvia sniffed in disgust. "She obviously went on to look for more promising prey, as far as I can see."

"So Kate didn't come from a background wealthy enough to suit you."

"I hardly matter, dear. She looked at you with stars in her eyes, thinking 'Easy Street.' A false assumption, which in all fairness needed to be corrected. While in your case, you do need to marry well enough that your path will be easier. With my connections, I can help you—"

"You can't use people like that."

"Think hard on this. You have the lovely Hastings girl waiting for you at the club. She can offer a beautiful, comfortable life, if you two can work things out. Or," Sylvia added with a gesture of distaste, "you can pursue the kind of woman who lies and has the worst possible background.

Put all of that law school education to good use and think rationally, for once."

"I'm doing that right now." He reached around her for the Mustang keys lying on the entryway table and strode to the door, where he hesitated with one hand on the frame. "Just to let you know, Sheila and I have been talking on the phone for the past hour. She doesn't want our so-called engagement any more than I do, and we've called it off. She decided she'd rather deal with her problems in her own way."

Sylvia stared at him as everything slowly clicked into place. Sheila Hastings's many anxious phone calls whenever Jared was here. Jared's lifelong, heartfelt need to help anyone in trouble. Sylvia struggled for a casual tone. "So, dear, when is her baby due?"

His eyes flared wide with surprise, but he said nothing.

"Is it yours?"

She could see the war of his emotions in the subtle changes in his expression—the desire to protect the girl's tarnished honor versus his innate need to be honest.

After a long moment, Jared finally shook his head. "No. She was terrified about facing her parents, but she finally decided to tell them. She's talking to them this morning." He stepped through the doorway.

"Wh-where are you going now?"

"Back to school, to see if I can find Kate and try to save the only relationship that ever mattered. I just hope you love me enough to wish me luck."

DECIDING TO TAKE A LEAP of faith and implementing it were two different things. Finding that Kate and her friends had moved to parts unknown set him back temporarily, but then Jared began a systematic search.

The building manager refused to say a word. The other residents either had never met the girls or had been on vague hi-in-the-hallway terms, and no one knew where they'd gone.

At the vet school, he lingered in the main foyer, hoping to catch a glimpse of Kate, Leesa or Deanna, but apparently they'd dropped off the face of the planet, and none of the other students were talking, either.

At the end of the day, when he caught a glimpse of his unshaven face and wild hair in the storefront window of a nearby pizza place, he finally understood why.

Someone behind him chuckled. "I'm not sure

if you look like a serial killer or something left over after a buffalo stampede. What happened to you?"

He turned to find one of Kate's classmates—a lanky guy named Phil—standing there with a pizza box and a liter of Coke. The pizza— probably a double pepperoni, given the amazing aroma wafting from the box—reminded Jared that he hadn't eaten since last night, and his stomach growled. "I've had kind of a rough day. Have you seen Kate?"

"That would depend on who's asking, and why." Phil's smile vanished. "What's it to you?"

"I just really want to find her, that's all."

Phil's eyes narrowed to a challenging glare. Jared was suddenly glad the burly kid had his arms full, because he looked as if he wanted to land a sucker punch on Jared's jaw.

"You're the guy who dumped her!"

"She dumped me. Where are you headed?"

"Dorm."

Jared eyed the box. An extra large, easily. "If I pay for half, want to share that pizza? Then I'll explain, and maybe you can help me out." He felt for his wallet. "It'd be worth an extra five."

"Ten."

"Seven, and that's final."

"Whatever." Phil turned and opened the box on

one of the tables set up outside the pizza place. "Help yourself. I bought too much, anyway."

Jared tossed a ten and a five on the table and picked up a steaming wedge of stuffed crust pepperoni, wrestling with the long ropes of mozzarella. "Kate dumped me, like I said. Big misunderstanding. I'm trying to find her to make things right, but she moved and no one can tell me where. Do you know?"

Phil snorted. "Why would I tell you?"

"Why not?"

"Her friend Leesa is a lab buddy of mine, and the last I heard, she thought you were lower than pond scum. I think she'd deck me if I told you." He chewed for a while. "Have you seen how powerful she is? I swear the girl could be a wrestler if she tried."

Jared grinned at the obvious admiration in his voice. "Can you ask her to get word to Kate for me? Tell her that we need to talk." He shoved the money across the table. "Tell her that I feel even *lower* than that pond scum, and just want to apologize."

Phil smiled around a mouthful of pizza. "You got it, but no guarantees. Leesa isn't a fan of yours…and from the sounds of it, she's got good cause."

WHEN HIS PHONE RANG the following night, Jared grabbed it on the second ring. At the sound of

Leesa's subdued voice, he closed his eyes in relief, but it still took nearly fifteen minutes and a lot of fast talking to convince her to share their new address.

"I'd better not regret this," she warned him. "I'm not sure it's a good idea at all. If you hurt Kate's feelings again, I swear you'll be one sorry dude."

He smiled into the phone, relieved and impatient to be on his way. "Believe me, Phil already warned me. I'll be there in a half hour."

He made it to the old, three-story house overlooking Lily Park in twenty minutes. The house had been divided into apartments, and he took the two inner flights of stairs two steps at a time. At 3-B he dragged in a deep breath and ran his hands through his hair, then rapped on the door.

He blinked when Kate opened the door herself, and just stared at her, forgetting to say hello.

She was thinner now, her cheekbones sharp and her eyes almost too large for her face. She didn't smile in welcome. "Leesa said you wanted something?"

"I…need to talk to you. Can I come in?"

She hesitated, then nodded and stepped aside. "The living room is to the left. There's no one else with you?"

"Just me."

"I heard you were engaged."

"Briefly. It was a mistake for both of us."

She sighed and led the way into the living room, where she motioned him to the couch and settled into a tattered upholstered chair across from him, tucking her legs beneath her. "Tough luck."

"No, good luck. The best."

"Seems sort of callous. Did you break the poor girl's heart?"

"I think she was even happier about the breakup than I was." He gave a single shake of his head. "My mother is the one with the broken heart, but then it was mostly her idea."

Kate laughed at that. "Let me get this straight. You let your *mother* handle your love life now?"

"Sounds pathetic, doesn't it? But it wasn't that. Sheila was on the rebound, and so was I. We connected through the country club back home, and our parents were absolutely thrilled. But it happened way too fast, and ended abruptly, too. My mother, unfortunately, thought it was a match made in heaven."

Kate eyed him. "You came all the way over here to tell me that? I really don't want to hear any updates about your romantic adventures."

"I came because I found out what my mother said to you at Thanksgiving."

She flinched.

"She had no business interfering, Kate. Nothing she said was true. I only wish I could turn back the clock and make that day disappear."

"Look, I appreciate that. But your latest failed romance doesn't mean you can bounce back here and start where you left off. And no matter what your mother said, I have my own reasons why you and I just won't work. Okay?"

She stood as if to usher him to the door, but he didn't budge. "You don't understand."

"I understand plenty," she shot back. "Good night, Jared. Have a good life."

CHAPTER TEN

KATE LEANED HER FOREHEAD against the door, her heart aching.

She hadn't expected to ever see Jared again, yet even six months after their breakup she'd still found herself looking for him at every turn. Foolishly thinking that every tall, dark-haired male student in the distance might be him. That every small black car would turn out to be his Mustang.

In her fantasy—one she'd try to dispel—he'd see her, and time would stand still for one long, aching moment. And then he'd come running, begging to come back. They'd be able to work things out, because all of the terrible things in her past wouldn't matter.

Reality was, no matter how he denied them, his mother's words still reverberated through her thoughts. And the cold facts remained. They were from different worlds, and her family background would have been an embarrassment, just as Sylvia Mathers said.

And there was nothing Kate could do to change it.

Even after she graduated from college and had DVM behind her name, it wouldn't be difficult for a reporter to dig up the sordid details of her past.

One of the bedroom doors squeaked and Leesa tentatively peeked out. "Is he gone? Can we come out now?"

Kate raised her arms wide. "Be my guest. The Big Scene is over."

"Humph." Deanna stepped into the small central hallway and folded her arms across her chest. "I still think we should've confronted him together. The three of us—inquisition style. You know—grill him for a while, then take him to his knees. What kind of guy walks out on one girl and suddenly gets engaged to the next one? Maybe he was two-timing you all along."

"We weren't exactly going steady."

"Yes, you were. Just not in so many words. You were together all the time."

Leesa stepped past Deanna and into the hallway. "I liked the guy, really. And I thought he was totally into Kate from the very start."

Kate bit her lower lip. "Then—"

A sharp knock sounded at the door and all three of them jumped. Leesa turned and peered through the security peephole. "Speak of the devil. Should we just ignore him?"

"Really mature, Leesa—he knows I'm here." Kate flipped the dead bolt. With her friends at her side, she swung the door open. "Forget something?"

"You." He looked at the three women, one by one. "And I want to argue my case."

No one moved.

"First, I wasn't the one who provided the damaging testimony to…uh…the plaintiff here over Thanksgiving. It was my mother, who didn't consult with me about my future plans, my current wishes or about my feelings for the woman in question. She was incorrect and, unfortunately, inappropriate in her remarks."

A sheepish smile played at the corner of his mouth. "Though believe me, I've never had any luck at trying to influence her, and neither did my late father."

When no one said anything, he held Kate's gaze with his own. "And I'd like to set the record straight. I didn't want to end our relationship, but you insisted. That failed engagement happened too fast. It was a classic case of rebound. But I wouldn't care if you had a rap sheet a mile long, or if your relatives belonged to the mob. I care about you. Not your family, not your past."

Kate cast a sideways glance at her roommates. Deanna stared at him with a dreamy expression.

Even Leesa seemed rapt. "Gosh, I think I'd take that explanation, Kate. Works for me."

Rolling her eyes, Kate grabbed his arm and led him down the stairs to the covered porch, where there'd be some privacy.

"Want my coat?" He brushed a strand of hair away from her cheek. "It's awfully chilly out here."

"This won't take a minute. Look, I really don't think—"

He rested his hands on her shoulders. "Then don't think. Just look at me, Kate. Tell me that you don't believe this could work. That you don't feel something deep inside…a rush of excitement when you see me, because I sure feel that every time I see you."

On the way down the stairs, she'd practiced the careful, logical words she should say. They were all swept away as soon as she looked up into his eyes. "I…"

"We've got our lives ahead of us, Kate, and right now I just can't imagine that life without you. Just give us another chance…please?"

"I…"

"Give it a try?"

After a moment's hesitation, she nodded and stepped into his arms for a heart-melting kiss.

What would it matter if they dated for a while? After graduation, he'd undoubtedly go to work for some fancy law firm in a big city and follow in his dad's footsteps. She'd end up in a vet practice somewhere out in the country.

And they wouldn't even last together that long, because the attainable grew boring, and love didn't last. He'd meet some gorgeous law student or a medical resident, and then he'd be gone.

She'd long since learned not to give her heart away.

Present Day

SOMEWHERE AT THE EDGES of Jared's consciousness, beyond the fog of pain, he sensed tension. Rushing footsteps. Anxious voices…his mother's sharp voice rising above the rest. *Sylvia?*

Clanging metal.

The rattle of wheels. And then he felt…

Alone.

Totally, helplessly alone; as if he were sinking back into a dark, bottomless sea.

The darkness was at once terrifying and a place of refuge from the pounding, intolerable pain that swelled and throbbed inside his head with every deafening beat of his heart.

Still, he tried to swim up out of the depths of that black velvet place that inexorably pulled him back. A place where nothing was familiar, yet somehow it offered the lure of total and everlasting peace.

He struggled to focus on a faint voice.

Familiar, yet completely foreign…drifting toward him through an incomprehensible world, spurring brief, fragile images of a child.

A slow dance in the moonlight.

Memories of love, and joy…and gut-wrenching grief.

A dim flicker of light appeared, then slithered away like an eel…too elusive to catch, leaving a fresh surge of bone-shattering pain ricocheting inside his skull.

He slipped back into the depths, giving himself to its dark embrace, letting reality fade away like sunlight filtering through the water as one dived deeper and deeper.

Oblivion offered respite from the confusion and pain that had been pressing on him from every side, threatening to smother him.

Had it been hours? Days? Months?

How long had he been like this?

Tires squealed. The deafening sound of twist-

ing, shearing metal exploded in his head, followed by the acrid smell of burning rubber. Gasoline. Then the searing flames of hell, and a woman's screams that went on, and on, and on...

The terrifying nightmare spun through him in a dizzying rush...then slowed, coiling around his heart like a cold, massive snake of guilt, squeezing tighter and tighter.

Oh, God. What have I done?

The Past

JARED PACED THE SIDEWALK in front of the big old house. He'd walked around the block twice, barely noticing the couples playing touch football over by the tennis courts, or the kids awkwardly rolling giant balls of snow into lopsided snowmen.

Barely aware of the mid-January sub-zero windchill that was dropping steadily as the sun lowered in the sky.

After seeing Kate every day for weeks, he should have found it easy to lope up that flight of stairs and knock on her door. But an inner voice held him back, repeating a litany that had been part of his life since the day his father died. *You know what your responsibilities are. To yourself, to your sister.*

Responsibility.

Duty.

At sixteen, he'd shouldered that and more without a second thought. At twenty-two, the choice no longer seemed so narrow. He would do everything he could to help, but not at the cost of a loveless marriage or a career he'd never wanted.

With a jerk of his shoulders, he pivoted and headed straight for the house, feeling drawn by an invisible force.

He came face-to-face with Kate at the front door.

Clearly surprised, she opened it wide and stepped out onto the porch. She dropped her backpack and, resting her hands on his shoulders, rose on her tiptoes to give him a swift kiss.

Before she could step back, he caught her in his arms and spun her around, then gave her a long, deep kiss until she sank against him. Breathless and weak-kneed himself, he finally tucked her head beneath his chin and held her in an embrace…and wished for the hundredth time that she would let their relationship move to the next level. Most girls would've pushed themselves for it to happen.

Kate always just grinned and stepped back, with gentle reminders about her future, her goals—adamant that she wasn't going to let anything stand in her way.

She tilted her head up at him. "I looked out and

saw your car a while ago, but you didn't come upstairs. I started to wonder if you'd gotten lost."

"I've been finding myself."

She laughed, her golden-brown eyes sparkling in the late-afternoon sun. "How New Age of you. If you were successful, we should probably head out to the library."

He shouldered her backpack and grabbed her hand. "Not quite yet. I need to show you something."

"But—"

"It's not far." He slanted a look at her. "I think you'll like it."

She gave him a questioning glance, but followed him to his car and got in after stowing her backpack in the backseat. "Give me a hint."

"Nope."

"Animate or inanimate?"

"Not telling." He started the car and turned up the heater, then popped in her favorite Bonnie Raitt CD.

"C'mon," she wheedled, giving his arm a playful punch. "I made fettuccini for you last night."

He sighed, not taking his eyes from the narrow, snowy streets. "Okay. It's both."

"It can't be!"

He lifted a shoulder. "That's your clue."

"You are not," she countered dryly, "very good at giving clues."

"Well, here's the next one." He turned up Oak and stopped in front of a small story-and-a-half stucco with overgrown evergreens crowding the front yard. A pathway carved through high snowbanks led to an arched door with a narrow, vertical glass window. "Come with me."

He rounded the car and opened her door, then steadied her with a hand on her arm as she climbed out of the car. He ushered her up the sidewalk.

"You know these people?"

"Not exactly."

Her mouth dropped open when he sorted through the keys on his ring and fitted one into the door lock. "Are…they expecting you?"

"Nope." He pushed the door open and waved her in. "I think they're probably in sunny Florida by now, happily enjoying their retirement."

Her mouth twitched, then she grinned. "You're *renting* this place? We'll practically be neighbors!"

They stepped into the small living room with dark hardwood floors and an old-fashioned archway leading into a small dining area. "This place is so cool."

"There's something else." He tipped his head toward a short hall leading through the center of the house to the rooms obviously remaining—a kitchen, bath and bedroom. "Lead the way."

She grinned mischievously. "I'm not *that* easy."

"Believe me, no one would ever accuse you of that. Go out the back door to the screened porch."

"A porch?" Her eyes lit up. "It just gets better and better."

Something rustled out on the porch when she touched the door handle. "I hope you don't have raccoons out there—they'll destroy your screens."

A yip sounded, followed by plaintive whines and a scrabbling at the door. She opened the door and knelt just in time to catch the blond ball of fur that launched itself at her. Overwhelmed by the wriggling mass of puppy, she fell back and scooted against the entryway wall, ruffling the pup's fur and laughing in delight at his kisses.

"You even got a dog. That's way, *way* cool." She held the pup up briefly, nose to nose. When she angled a look up at Jared, her eyes held a sheen of tears. "He's gorgeous. And he's even a golden retriever—just like the figurine you gave me."

"A mix, I hear. He came from the humane shelter. One look at him and I was a goner."

Tired after his burst of exuberance, the pup curled up in her lap. "He's absolutely perfect. And it's all the better because you saved his life. You're now my official hero."

Jared hunkered down next to her. "I found this

house to rent and just couldn't pass it up. It's close to the vet school for you, and just a few blocks from the campus bus for me. I figure that we spend an awful lot of time going back and forth to see each other, and things could be a lot more simple."

Her smile faded. "It's all great, Jared. Really. But if you thought I would move in, well…"

"That's where Murphy comes in. I figured I might stand a better chance if you were offered two guys for the price of one. What do you think?"

Her eyes widened, and her hands stilled on the pup's soft golden fur. "I…I'm not exactly sure what you're saying."

"I knew I'd have trouble with this, so I had a talk with Murph, and he said he'd handle it. He has a present for you."

She gave a nervous laugh as she glanced around the hallway. "I hope it doesn't involve paper towels and Pine-Sol."

"Not that kind of present, though he and I had a talk about that, too. He promises he's going to try really hard to be good." Jared reached over to ruffle the pup's baby-soft coat. "Check his collar. I could be wrong, but I think he said he'd put the present there."

"If it's edible, I don't think I'm interested."

"I don't know. Better take a look, don't you think?"

She stilled, then took a shaky breath and gently felt Murphy's collar. "Maybe he lost it."

"I sincerely hope not. Check a little closer."

She gently fingered the collar, then released the catch and lifted it away. The overhead light caught the piercing sparkle of a slender band tied to the buckle, and at that she froze.

"Strange rabies tag," Jared murmured when she didn't say anything. He felt his pulse pick up an unsteady beat. "What does it say?"

"I…" She blinked and rubbed at her eyes with the back of her wrist. "I think Murphy is a little young to be looking for this kind of commitment."

"He's just the right age. And so are we, Kate."

"Are we?" She shot a brief glance at him, her voice tinged with panic. "I never thought… I mean, what will your mother say? You know she'll hate this. And you have so much school left. So do I, and…"

Jared lifted the sleeping pup from her lap and set him on the braided rug in front of the door, then took her hand and they rose to face each other.

Looking into her eyes, he saw worry and confusion, with a touch of fear, but he also saw the longing that matched his own, and that gave him the courage to continue. "I love you, Kate. From the moment we met, I felt this connection that just took over my heart, and I know it will never leave. When you broke up with me, I thought the world had ended. Now—it's like anything in the world is possible, but only if it's with you."

"Your *family*."

"I don't have to be Senator Ellsworth Mathers II to find success, Kate…though there's no reason I couldn't, whether I'm with you or not. My mother was dead wrong about you…about us. And she can't make decisions about where you and I go with this relationship."

She leaned her forehead against his chest. "I wish that were true. But I don't want to come between you and your family, ever."

"I love you, Kate. Why spend the next years of college apart when we could be together?" His heart lifted when she didn't immediately disagree. "We could get married next week. The week after that."

"It's not that simple."

"Will your family disapprove?"

At that, she wryly shook her head. "They wouldn't care."

"Well, mine *will* accept this." He kissed the tip of her nose. "They'll come to love you, just as I do. I promise."

"I love you, too, more than I could ever say." She silently looked up at him for so long that he feared the rest of her answer. "I just hope you're not wrong."

CHAPTER ELEVEN

KATE HELD UP HER HAND to stare at the ring on her finger, shifting her hand in the candlelight of the church to catch the sparkles.

It had been his grandmother's ring, and she could well imagine the value of it. She had little knowledge about fine jewelry, but it seemed to have perfect clarity and the brilliant cut caught fire in the sun. Jared had kept it in his safe-deposit box at the bank since the day his grandfather gave it to him after the death of Jared's grandmother.

She could only imagine what Sylvia thought about a treasured family heirloom falling into such disreputable hands. Jared had called her the evening Kate said "Yes," and she'd heard only his side of the conversation, but the woman had been anything but pleased.

So be it.

Perhaps Kate's dreams of having an extended

family, with dinners on Sunday and warm, happy holidays together, would never come true, but she and Jared had each other, and her happiness had grown with every passing day.

And what had started as an engagement had rocketed forward in a white heat, with neither of them seeing any point in delaying beyond the first available date at the church.

"You're sure you want to go through with this?" she asked quietly. "I know it isn't the sort of fairy-tale wedding you would've had if you were marrying someone else."

"You are my fairy tale," he whispered back. "I don't need anything else."

And it was true for her, too.

The small chapel stood near the college. Built of massive, rough-hewn stone back in the 1800s, it smelled of candles and age and crumbling hymnals. Harsh late-afternoon February sunlight filtered through a dozen intricately cut, jewel-toned stained-glass windows on the west side of the church, bathing the heavy pews in glowing light, the flickering candles adding a touch of intimacy.

Only Deanna, Leesa and Phil were present, but the elderly minister smiled beneficently on them all and delivered a warm message about love and commitment. And his wife, a frail old dear with violet hair and hands roped with veins played the organ with ethereal grace.

Closing her eyes, Kate imagined a church full of flowers and well-wishers. But none of that would have made the day more special than it already was as she stood at Jared's side, looking up into his dark, handsome face as he spoke his vows.

Sure, they were young. Broke. Had years of school left. But with this kind of soul-deep love, how could anything go wrong?

Present Day

SYLVIA GLARED at the doctor, the monitors around her bed and the young nurse hovering just beyond arm's reach. Her angry gaze settled on Kate next and hardened to pure steel.

"Leave it to you to cause trouble," she hissed. "Even now, with my son so badly injured."

"Dr. Kate didn't make the call, ma'am," the nurse ventured, shooting a wary glance between Kate and the staff physician, Dr. Walters. "The ICU nurses did."

Sylvia waved her off like a troublesome fly, her anger palpable. "Tell these people to let me go at once. I need to be with Jared, not wasting my time like this."

Dr. Walters cleared his throat. "You fainted, Mrs. Mathers. Your blood pressure was just 70 over 54, and your pulse was too fast. We want to run an EKG to make sure nothing's wrong before we release you. Have you had any chest pain?"

"No."

"Shortness of breath?"

"No." The nurse moved forward to pull the blood pressure cuff from its holder on the wall above the head of the bed, but Sylvia swung her legs off the gurney and batted her away. "I'm refusing medical care. Is that clear enough?"

The doctor frowned. "I really think we should—"

"Let me *be*." But Sylvia's face turned ashen as she slid off the gurney and her knees buckled.

Dr. Walters caught her under one arm and the nurse under the other. They gently backed her into a chair where she slumped forward, a sheen of perspiration forming on her forehead.

"Are you her daughter?" Walters asked.

Kate shook her head. "Daughter-in-law. Her daughter, Julia, is trying to arrange the soonest possible flight here from New York. Sylvia's son—my husband—is a patient in the ICU."

"We need to run some tests. I'm guessing we might even want to keep her overnight." As an afterthought, he turned to Sylvia and appeared to carefully choose his words. "I'm concerned about your heart. We certainly don't want to take any chances now, do we?"

"Humph." But this time, she didn't argue.

"Whatever it takes. We just want her to be safe." Kate reached over and rested a hand on Sylvia's shoulder. "It's time for me to go sit with Jared for a few minutes, but then I'll be back."

Beneath her hand, Kate felt the old woman stiffen. Alarmed, she bent closer. "Are you okay? Does your chest hurt?"

But it wasn't pain reflected in Sylvia's eyes. It was the first hint of fear and loneliness the woman had ever revealed, though Kate knew she was too proud and stubborn to ever admit it.

"This is the place to be if you're not feeling well, and you're in good hands. I promise I'll let you know immediately if there are any changes with Jared, okay?"

When Sylvia responded with a single, curt nod, Kate hurried back to the ICU and took her place at Jared's bedside.

He lay there without moving, and his thick, dark eyelashes didn't even flutter when she took one of his hands in hers. She shot an anxious look at the monitor stands on the other side of the bed.

The fluorescent green lines continued to slide across the screens; his heart, pulse and respiration were as steady as before.

One of the nurses—Barbara S. on her name pin—silently appeared at her shoulder. "The surgeon was back in while you were gone. The pressure in Jared's skull hasn't gone down as much as he hoped, so he added another med to the IV that should help."

Alarm flashed through Kate. "I want to talk to that doctor."

Barbara smiled. "He thought as much. He's doing rounds, but he'll be back. He said to tell you it's not unusual to put a patient into a barbiturate-induced coma for a while to help bring that cranial pressure down."

Kate mentally reviewed the complications of barbiturate use in animal medicine and guessed at the similarities in humans. "But the risks… Is he aware of the risks?"

"Altered heart function and liver damage are possibilities, but of course we are monitoring your husband very closely, and he won't be on it for very long."

Soothing words for family.

Generalities.

Comfort.

Optimism.

Heaven knew how many times she'd handled distraught families just that gently during the critical illness of a beloved pet. But what Kate needed now was for Jared to open his eyes and look at her—for him to know his own name, and where he was, and what he'd had for breakfast.

"No matter what else happened yesterday, we can work through it," she whispered softly. "Come back to me, please. Come back."

The nurse slipped away and left Kate to sit with him alone. But despite what Barbara had said, Kate knew there was still a very real possibility that Jared wouldn't survive this endless night…or that he might never be the same.

And, once again, she began to pray.

By SEVEN O'CLOCK in the morning, Kate was exhausted after running between Sylvia's room and the ICU.

"Mr. Mathers will be fine if you want to slip home for a while." Marie, the perky redheaded nurse who'd just arrived for first shift, checked her watch. "I don't expect the docs to come around for at least another hour, maybe more."

At the thought of a good, hot shower and a chance to check in at the vet clinic, Kate nodded. "You've got my cell number?"

Marie nodded. "Taped to the front of your husband's chart, as well as on the records inside. If he so much as looks at me cross-eyed, I'll give you a call."

"Or even if he just opens his eyes, let me know. He hasn't stirred a bit."

"And we don't expect him to. Not yet." The young nurse fairly vibrated with energy as she shelved the chart and bustled from the nurses' counter to Jared's bay, where she examined the bags of IV saline and meds hanging above his bed. "But I'll call you, I promise."

"ARE YOU SURE you don't want me to come in with you?"

Casey shook her head and managed a smile. "I know you have to get back to work in Madison, and the ICU would only admit family members, anyway. Thanks so much for everything, though."

Deanna bit her lower lip, as if worrying over just how much to say. "It…will be a shock, seeing your dad. It was for me when my dad had a heart attack. All the tubes and wires and monitors were sort of scary."

"I know." Casey opened her car door, then leaned over to give her mother's old friend a quick kiss on the cheek. "You've been the best. Thanks."

She fetched her duffel and backpack out of the backseat of the SUV, nodded in farewell, then trudged through the automatic doors of the E.R.

Even before she'd got on the plane, fear and dread had been churning through her stomach over the upcoming scene with her parents. Arriving to find Deanna waiting at the airport instead of Mom, and hearing the awful news about Dad, had made everything a thousand times worse.

The nurse at the desk waved her over to the elevators.

Outside, the air was crisp and sweet with the scent of a northern spring, and the early-morning light was still soft with a wispy mist that intensified the lush green landscape of the hospital grounds. Inside, the bright lighting and the smell of disinfectant made her eyes burn as she sidestepped a woman scrubbing the floor and stepped into the elevator.

She hadn't let herself think about this moment.

She'd politely refused to talk about it with Deanna.

But now it was here. The elevator doors were opening. And straight down the long hallway, she could see the ICU sign on a set of double doors.

Her hands shook as she hiked her backpack higher up on her shoulder and took one slow step after another toward those doors. How bad was he? Would he even make it? Would he even know her?

A single, hot tear slid down her cheek as she tried to imagine life without him…his playful teasing, the truly awful jokes that sent Mom and her into gales of laughter, because they were so silly. The sweet gifts he bought at the most unexpected times, just because.

She didn't deserve a great dad like him. Not now. And how could she even begin her explanations when he and Mom were already dealing with so much?

Taking a deep breath, she pushed on the door and found herself in yet another hallway that opened up into a visitors' lounge, with doors marked ICU— Limited Admittance straight ahead.

As if by magic—or an unseen alarm—a stocky nurse came through the doors and smiled. "You must be Casey. We've been watching for you, dear. Come on in."

"Is he… Is my dad…okay?"

"He's sleeping very soundly right now, thanks to some of the medications. But you can go in and sit with him awhile."

Nervous, Casey forced herself to follow the nurse into the ICU to a curtained section where she could see only the end of the bed and the outline of some sort of frame to keep the bedding away from Dad's burned flesh.

The nurse smiled sympathetically and rested a hand on Casey's arm. "It's hard, I know. But his color is good, and he's a strong man. The doctors say that he might even be able to go home in a few weeks. Maybe less."

Casey nodded to her in thanks and stepped around the bed to the chair placed near Dad's head.

Just as the nurse had said, he looked as if he were simply sleeping—except for the stark white bandaging on his head, such a contrast to his dark hair, and all of the tubes trailing from the IV bags hanging on a tall pole.

The sounds of a compressor and the soft beeps and chirps of the various monitors were deafening against the hushed silence of this place.

Prickly tears filled her eyes and she scrubbed them away. He looked so alone, so defenseless. Up close, she now saw the tiny sutures marching up the side of his lean face and the lines of stress at his mouth and eyes.

"Oh, Daddy," she whispered, touching his still, cool hand where it lay on top of the covers at his side. His complete lack of response frightened her and she jerked her hand away. "Why isn't Mom with you?"

Of course, her mother was at her clinic 24/7,

and her father was always immersed in his law practice. Last summer, he'd rarely come home before ten at night, with all the extra hours he donated to the free clinic. How close were they, if they hardly ever saw each other anymore?

The thought filled her with a sense of loss over the family they'd once been, back when the house was filled with laughter and the weekends were spent on outings together.

"I'm here, Daddy. I don't know if you can hear me, but I need to talk to you so badly."

She tentatively took his hand in hers once again and held her breath, waiting for his fingers to curl around hers and squeeze, acknowledging her. Wishing Mom would suddenly stride into the room and announce that everything would be all right.

Though maybe it was better this way…a chance to be with him alone for a while. A chance to unburden her heart, even if he couldn't really hear her.

"Oh, Daddy," she whispered. "I'm so sorry about your accident. You've got to get better. You've just got to."

A nurse peeked around the curtain at the foot of his bed. "Just a few more minutes, dear."

Casey nodded and turned back to her father's still form. "And there's something else…something I've got to tell you, but I don't know how. You and Mom always wanted the best for me. And you've given me so much—"

One of the monitors by the bed sounded a shrill alarm and suddenly there were nurses everywhere, jostling for position at the bed, reaching for something on the IV pole.

"We need to help your father," one of them said in a low, urgent voice. "Go back to the visitors' lounge."

Hurried footsteps arrived, followed by a cart rattling across the floor, and three more medical personnel burst into the small area. Casey stumbled backward, straining to see her father's face one more time as guilt flooded through her.

Had he really heard her? Had her words stressed him out, tipping the balance in his already precarious state? A wave of grief swamped her. And why wasn't anyone here with him? The nurses had made her leave, and with no sign of Mom or Grandma anywhere, was he going to die alone?

She blindly made her way back to the lounge, barely able to see through her hot tears. An old man sat hunched over in a chair to one side. He lifted his head briefly in alarm when she appeared at the door, then sank back with a heavy sigh and dropped his head over his folded hands.

So someone else was here, too, awaiting bad news.

She managed a weak smile in his direction, though he didn't look up as she passed on her way to the far end of the room. The bitter irony of it all hit her as she settled at the edge of a chair, her eyes pinned on the open doorway and a sick feeling of dread pressing in on her from every side.

During the entire flight home, she'd been nearly overwhelmed with anxiety over the conversation to come. But now, the ruin of her own life seemed as inconsequential as a speck of dust.

CHAPTER TWELVE

KATE GLANCED AT HER WATCH and unlocked the back door of her clinic, stepped inside and locked it behind her.

There'd been a time when she would have left it open to the crisp early-morning breeze, happy to savor the sharp scent of pine and the faint spring fragrance of lilacs. When she would've been comfortable with unlocked doors and open windows, knowing that her small town had always been safe. Now, her first thought was to protect herself and her clinic.

How could everything be going so terribly wrong?

She flipped on the hall lights and felt a moment of peace at the familiar sounds of the clinic. From the moment she opened the door, a cacophony of barking erupted from the kennel room to the left, answered by the yowls of a disgruntled patient in the neighboring room reserved for cats.

Across the hall, where the birds, reptiles and pocket pets were housed, a cockatiel whistled sharply.

Amy would be here in an hour to begin her kennel duties before taking over the front desk at nine. Though Kate needed to get back to the hospital as soon as possible, it felt good to be in this familiar world, alone for a few minutes, with no questions, no expressions of sympathy.

She needed to check on her surgery cases.

Draw labs on the retriever still on IVs, recovering after consuming an entire bag of chocolates, to see if he could finally go home.

Examine the feline emergency C-section.

Everything else—all the appointments for today, and the three or four elective surgeries—Amy would need to cancel if she hadn't done so already.

Even being away from the hospital for less than an hour had Kate feeling jittery, as if a strong magnetic force was pulling her back, but thankfully there hadn't been any calls from the ICU since she'd been gone.

Yet.

On her way into the kennel room, she reached for the comforting presence of the cell phone in her jacket pocket. Startled at its absence, she quickly searched her other pockets, her purse, then ran back out to her car.

Had she left it at home, where she'd gone for a quick shower and a change of clothes? Back at the hospital? Her anxiety swelled. What if someone had tried to call her about Jared?

Calm down, she told herself sternly. *They do have the house and clinic numbers in Jared's chart. Everything is all right.*

Still, she hurried to the front office to check the answering machine and felt her heart stumble at the blinking light. *Please—no bad news. Please.* Her hands trembling, she pressed the button.

A call from a pharmaceutical sales rep, promising to be in late this afternoon.

Lucille Clark asking about her dog Percy, the cruciate ligament surgery Kate had done yesterday—probably at the very time Jared was getting in his car for his fateful trip.

Getting in his car with another woman at his side, an insidious inner voice whispered. *A woman who was dead less than an hour later.*

Oh, Lord—what on earth happened?

Biting her lip, Kate fought back a surging sense of loss and betrayal and grief as she hit the button again.

A reminder about the county veterinary

meeting tomorrow night and a fervent plea for her to run for an office this year.

And then…the small, heartbroken voice of her daughter.

"Mom. Where are you? Why aren't you here?" Her voice caught. "Daddy—he doesn't look so good. The nurses came running in and they made me leave and…and I'm *scared*."

Oh, God, please not now—don't let him die with Casey there alone.

Grabbing the keys from the rack at the back door of the clinic, Kate ran to her car. She hesitated for just a heartbeat, then climbed behind the wheel. Had she locked the clinic? Surely she had…and Amy would arrive in less than an hour, at any rate. It would be okay, and she had no minutes to waste.

She reached up to adjust the rearview mirror before backing out and caught a glimpse of her tension-ravaged face, almost unrecognizable from the one she saw in the bathroom mirror every morning. She floored the accelerator on the two-mile stretch of country road leading into town.

What would life be like without Jared at her side?

Long ago, she'd been entranced by his dark, handsome face, his intelligence and wit. But over the years, those superficial feelings had deepened into so much more despite the rocky times—the terrible times when there'd been no glimmer of hope that they'd still be together in five or ten or twenty years.

And yet recently, they'd somehow drifted apart.

Please—help him make it through this so he can come home again. Give us another chance, so we can make things right. Like back in college, when it was just us against the world...

The Past

"My mother has asked us to dinner." Jared hesitated. "In honor of our marriage."

Kate felt a shiver crawl up her spine at the prospect of facing Sylvia Mathers over dinner. After Jared called her with the news of their elopement, Sylvia's cold silence had hung a pall over their marriage.

Kate startled whenever her phone rang, expecting a diatribe.

Jared had been subtly withdrawn, perhaps dealing with his own demons regarding the sense of responsibility his mother had so ruthlessly drummed into him.

During the few times they'd met, Kate had found the woman to be cold and unpleasant, and she'd figured careful distance from Sylvia was probably the safest course. But Jared... Was he having second thoughts? Did he wish he hadn't made such a rash, crazy decision regarding his entire future?

"Well? What do you think—can we make it tonight? It's at the Starfire Room. The food is excellent there."

At the hope in his eyes, there was no way she could refuse, even with a pharmacology test tomorrow and a paper due on Friday. "I'll bet you miss your sister," Kate said, trying for a genuine smile. "Of course we should go."

Jared's shoulders relaxed and he wrapped his arms around her in a tight embrace. "I love you," he whispered against her ear.

Her dread over the dinner slipped into a whole different sort of anticipation—one that made her toes tingle and filled her with desire for him that only grew stronger with every passing month. She'd never imagined having this kind of love in her life. The feeling of being cared for. Cherished. Desired.

"Want to show me how much?" she teased, grabbing his hand as she stepped away. "I'll bet we have time. Plenty of time."

"Think so?" One eyebrow cocked, he appeared to consider the possibility for a long moment.

Then he lifted her in his arms and spun her around, and awkwardly managed the bedroom door, only to have them both collapse on the bed in a tangle of arms and legs and laughter.

That they lost track of time, lost in passion and hunger and unending delight in each other, didn't matter until the moment Kate walked into the restaurant holding Jared's hand and found Sylvia waiting, her face a mask of anger.

"You're *late*."

The imposing man standing next to her, a briefcase in hand, nodded at Jared. "Good to see you again, son."

"Lionel Norwood, I'd like you to meet my wife, Kate." Jared looked down at Kate and gave her hand a squeeze. "Lionel has been our family lawyer for years."

The man was impeccably dressed, with a cool, regal air. She felt her palms grow damp and a cold sweat start to trickle down her spine. *This wasn't going to be good.* "Nice to meet you."

A waiter appeared and ushered them to a corner with a spectacular night view of the Twin Cities. With a complex array of crystal goblets at each place setting and shimmering centerpieces of silver and crystal, the dark restaurant was lit by candlelight and glittered like a thousand stars.

None of the nearby tables were occupied, which afforded a measure of privacy. By accident, or design?

Kate slid into the chair pulled back for her by the waiter and looked up to find Sylvia silently watching her with a smug, tight smile.

Jared acknowledged his mother with a nod before turning to Lionel. "Good to see you again. I'm a little surprised, though."

Lionel canted his head slightly. "Family business is my business, since your father passed away. And, of course, your mother and I have been friends for many years."

"So, is this business or pleasure?" Jared's voice now held a hint of steel. "I understood Kate and I were simply coming to a nice little family dinner. Just the four of us. Where's Julia?"

"She's at a sleepover, so your mother asked me to join you." Lionel accepted a sample of wine from a waiter bearing a tray and wine bottle, a white napkin draped over his arm.

Kate watched as he considered it, then requested something from another year.

Back home, there'd been gallon jugs that disappeared all too quickly, and the results had devastated her family. No doubt there were just as many alcoholics at this end of the economic spectrum, but it would be achieved with a gloss of class and at considerably higher cost.

There was something all too familiar in Lionel's complexion and manner that hinted he might be one of them.

"So," Sylvia said after the waiter poured her wine. "We've come to this." She lifted her glass in a halfhearted, mocking salute.

Kate stiffened.

"A reason to celebrate," Jared interjected smoothly. "Kate and I are lucky we found each other, and I couldn't be happier."

The waiter poured for Jared, as well, then hesitated at Kate's side, but she declined the wine.

"I'm sure *she* is celebrating," Sylvia snapped. "What a lucky, lucky girl. I'm just glad my Julia isn't here to witness this disaster."

"Sylvia." Lionel leveled a warning look at her, tempered by a faint smile, then directed his attention to Kate. "This marriage has come as a complete shock to Mrs. Mathers, as you might imagine."

What answer could there be to that? It was the truth, yet the negative connotation was crystal clear.

"Maybe you'd better direct your comments to me," Jared said. "Though I don't believe we'll be staying much longer."

"As I remember, you especially enjoyed the

porterhouse here on your twenty-first birthday…
the two-inch-thick cut with the herbed butter,"
Lionel said mildly. "And I imagine Kate would
love it, too. Don't rush off. This dinner is my
treat."

From somewhere across the room wafted the incredible aroma of some sort of steak—perhaps that
very same kind—and Kate's mouth watered. The
closest she'd been to a steak in the last six months
had been cattle on the hoof at the vet school and
all-beef hot dogs. Her stomach started to growl.
Embarrassed, she folded her arms over her belly.

Another waiter appeared at Lionel's side, and
after a brief conversation regarding the chef's rec-
ommendations, the lawyer ordered for everyone.

Over escargot and a creamy leek soup, the conversation turned to law school and the most advantageous law firms in the city for new grads.

Over the melt-in-your-mouth, buttery porterhouse steak for everyone except Sylvia, who chose
a salad, the conversation veered into old family
friends, politics and Senator Mathers's former
cronies…many of whom had retired.

With every passing minute, Kate felt less
visible, despite Jared's valiant efforts to include
her in the conversation. Futile efforts, because she
knew none of the people and none of the situa-

tions, and the pointed direction of the conversation was clearly meant to illustrate exactly that.

When the settings were cleared and the dessert menu offered, Kate politely declined and excused herself for the ladies' room, where she splashed some cold water on her wrists and tried to will away the growing headache that had started the moment she and Jared arrived.

Sylvia showed up a minute later, her expression triumphant, and Kate's heart sank.

"I thought I'd give Lionel and Jared a few minutes to discuss private matters." Sylvia gave a delicate shrug. "I know young men are so much more likely to accept advice from someone other than their mother, even if the information is all the same. A pity, really."

Sylvia stood between Kate and the exit, and trying to walk out would not only be disrespectful, but mean brushing against her. "Does…he have good advice, then?"

"Lionel is telling him what I am going to tell you, my dear." Sylvia folded her arms across her chest. "I do hope you have the backbone to hear me out."

Kate's heart sank.

"I told you already that there is no money. No security blanket to be had by marrying into this family. Our family 'fortune,' such as it is, is tied up in property that not only is heavily in debt with a second mortgage, but is heavily taxed. The only way Jared can hope to hold on to it is by becoming a very, very successful man. Do you understand this at all?"

A sharp retort died on Kate's lips. Despite her biting tone, the older woman's hands trembled and there was a hint of desperation in her eyes.

"His sister is ten years old. An advantageous marriage for Jared would've ensured that she could receive an education at a good private college, where she'd have a better chance to marry well. It would've ensured that I could continue to stay in my home." Sylvia's eyes glittered with angry tears. "His former fiancée is a sweet, intelligent girl. Did you know that her dad owns a chain of upscale department stores? Marriage to her would have been Jared's golden ticket…would have made his entire future."

"But what about Jared? His happiness?"

"His happiness?" Sylvia snorted. "Any young man his age would be delighted to have unlimited access to sex, and for that privilege, they convince themselves they're madly 'in love.' I'm sure he's quite the happy camper right now. But he's thinking with his hormones, not his head."

"It isn't just about…that."

"No? Then you tell me how happy he'll be when his old friends pass him by. When his friends and cousins are living exceedingly comfortable lives, while he's in some two-bit law practice without the right connections. Or when his sister graduates from a state college, if she's lucky enough to earn enough scholarships." Sylvia's mouth twisted. "I tried to tell you all of this already, but you wouldn't listen. And now you've snared my only son with your selfish little schemes. I only hope Lionel can talk some sense into him before it's too late."

Kate suddenly felt faint. "T-too late?"

"Too late to try for an annulment, so we can clean up this mess as quickly as possible." Sylvia leveled a contemptuous look at her. "Before you come up with any other complications so you can hang on to your foolish dreams."

CHAPTER THIRTEEN

"AN ANNULMENT," Kate said, two weeks later, keeping her voice flat and unemotional. "Your mother wanted you to pursue an annulment before 'something happened.' And now something has. I guess you made a big mistake, not listening to Lionel and her."

Jared stilled, staring at her across their small kitchen table. "We stood together against them, didn't we? We're both still in college, with 4.0 GPAs. No matter what they said, we're going to succeed. So what's wrong?"

She met his steady gaze, reading the love and determination in his beautiful, smoky gray eyes. Knowing it might change in a minute if she gathered enough courage to tell him.

And the two more years of vet school after this one, then the surgical residency she'd planned on long before she'd even started school. What about that? Now her future stretched ahead, down the same dark road her mother had been on during her own life, and the thought of it twisted Kate's insides into a painful mass of tension.

She turned away and braced her hands on the kitchen counter. "I'm pregnant."

"Be serious. Tell me what's really wrong." He moved to stand behind her and clasped his hands in front of her waist to pull her close. "Don't even think about what my mother and Lionel said."

She bowed her head. "I never once missed one of my pills. Never, ever. They're supposed to be so reliable. But I've been queasy every morning for the last week, and I finally went out to buy one of those kits at the drugstore."

He rested his chin on top of her head. "And?"

"The strip turned blue. I can't believe it. We had everything planned so well. We'd finish school. We'd each set up a practice in a perfect little town somewhere." She was babbling, and she just couldn't stop. "We'd get ourselves established, and in a few years we'd have a nice house and would start thinking about a family. Not now. Dear Lord, not now."

"You *are* serious."

"Am I laughing?"

After a long silence, Jared dropped his chin to

her shoulder and rested his cheek against hers. "Tell me how you feel about this. Really."

"Scared. Worried. Confused." She swallowed hard. "Afraid of what you're going to say next."

Another silence stretched so long that she finally squeezed her eyes shut and gathered the remnants of her courage. "Your mom told me how ending your other engagement cost you a very advantageous marriage. How that will hurt your future. Or your sister's. And now…now this. I am so, so sorry. If…if you want your freedom, I'll understand. I can be out of here in a few hours, and—"

"Stop." His voice was low and fierce. "Unless that's what you really want."

"I know you're an honorable guy. It's one of the things I love about you. But you don't want to saddle yourself with a pregnant wife at the age of twenty-two."

"Just tell me one thing. Do you want to keep this baby?"

Aghast, she pulled away and turned to face him. "You don't need to even ask that question. I may not have experience with living in anything but a dysfunctional family, but there's no way I could ever end this life inside me. And there's no way I could ever give it up. So you see? This is a good chance for you to leave—before things get messy and complicated."

He swore softly under his breath. "You don't know me at all if you think I'd walk out on you. I'm your *husband*."

"And those things can be fixed. Just ask your friend Lionel."

Jared rested his hands on her shoulders. "There's nothing I need to ask him. It's you and me, babe—now and forever."

Her heart lifted on an ember of hope. "Really?"

He sighed with obvious relief. "We can make it. It'll maybe be a little tough for a few years, but hey—we've got scholarships and good loans, and with our part-time jobs…" He kissed the tip of her nose. "We're in this together for the long haul. And hey—this way, we'll be young enough to really enjoy our family."

She leaned against him, absorbing his warmth, savoring the solid muscle of his chest. Was it possible that things could work out? "I love you," she whispered against his shirt. "There couldn't be a more wonderful guy than you in the entire world."

He rocked her in his arms, as if slow dancing to music that only he could hear. "You and I are more alike than you know. Neither of us had it easy as kids. But we're going to do this right."

THE NEXT EIGHT MONTHS passed in a blur. Late-night study sessions. Tests and papers and labs. Spring term followed by summer school, and then the start of the fall semester. By then, Kate felt as unwieldy as a Holstein ready to deliver triplets.

The summer job she'd started in June at a nearby drugstore had helped keep groceries on the table, but now unseasonably hot and humid September weather had descended. The air conditioner at the store couldn't keep up, and even with the fans blowing and the windows open at home she felt miserably hot and sticky. She spent more and more hours at the library, just trying not to melt.

She'd been able to hide her pregnancy until this month with baggy flannel shirts over loose overalls—a common uniform for ag students on campus, luckily. But T-shirts were more revealing, and the manager had frowned at her today, then muttered something about cutting her hours.

Lifting boxes in the back storeroom probably hadn't been the best idea, but she'd been desperate to prove that she could still pull her own weight.

With temperatures approaching ninety and the humidity at least that high, even the library didn't provide enough respite, so she'd gone home to study.

She stretched, glancing at the clock and wishing Jared was home. But he'd gone to a two-day law conference in Chicago and wouldn't return until tomorrow night. Lucky guy—conference hotels were invariably air-conditioned to almost chilly, which would feel just about right, today.

She winced as a muscle cramp tightened across her lower back.

Despite lifting those boxes earlier, she'd been careful to avoid doing anything that might endanger the baby.

Another muscle spasm radiated across the same area. More intense this time—and a frisson of alarm shot through her.

It was too early. The doctor at the free clinic had given her a due date four weeks from now.

And worse, Jared wasn't in town.

She swallowed a bitter laugh as images from recent TV commercials flashed through her thoughts.

Perfect, sunlit nurseries.

Doting grandparents, smiling into a lace-festooned bassinet, hugging the daughter who had given them a precious grandchild.

There'd be none of that for her.

When she'd first called her mother to tell her about the pregnancy, Francine had blearily said it was bad news and would ruin Kate's life.

Sylvia, her usual friendly and loving self, had

been appalled at this additional complication that would ruin her precious son's future. She'd been coldly polite over Easter and the Fourth of July, and she'd never called for any warm and happy chats about the baby, though Jared always brought the subject up anyway, each time they saw her. Julia—wide-eyed and subdued—had clearly heard their mother's diatribes at home and kept her own careful distance from them.

Nope, it was just the two of them, and now Jared wasn't even here. But this was just a simple muscle spasm, nothing more. It had to be that.

There'd be no use in calling Sylvia or her own mother.

And for the first time in her life, Kate knew she'd come up against something she couldn't face alone.

ALONE CERTAINLY NEEDED definition.

Her contractions started in earnest an hour later, then rapidly escalated to a steady eight minutes apart. By three o'clock in the morning, she gave up and took Murphy to the neighbor's place, then drove herself to the hospital, hoping she'd be sent home at least until Jared's return in the evening.

The nurse in the E.R. didn't appear very sympathetic as she ordered Kate into a wheelchair and called for a volunteer to take her upstairs. "You want to wait another fourteen hours? You'll be a momma by then."

The nurses upstairs were even less encouraging about a delay, and ten minutes later, Kate was gowned and admitted after making a quick call home and leaving a message on the machine.

The bright lights of the hospital had seemed warm and welcoming when she arrived, and she'd felt a momentary sense of relief.

The labor and delivery rooms bustled with activity and people. Nurses. Nursing students. A flock of residents who looked even younger than her, and who were probably in the first days of their OB rotation, given their nervous gestures and surreptitious glances at the pocket-size references crammed into their lab coats.

Lots of people, yet she'd never felt more alone.

Not so fast, little one, she whispered under her breath. *Maybe your daddy can still get here in time.*

But four hours later, her contractions were coming hard and fierce, and she was ready to do anything to have the baby come now, whether Jared was here or not.

Every so often a herd of people in white coats trooped into her room to listen to the baby's heartbeat and to check her IV, blood pressure and dilation—which had gone exactly nowhere.

Three centimeters at four o'clock in the morning, then six at ten o'clock.

By midafternoon, the doctor started a Pitocin drip. At five, she came back and broke Kate's water, then began murmuring to the nurses about starting Nubain for the pain, and Kate first heard the words *epidural* and *C-section.*

An hour later, a different nurse came in with a bright smile. "We're doing a quick ultrasound, and then the doc is coming in so you two can talk."

Exhausted, Kate concentrated on her breathing, trying not to steel herself against the searing crescendo of yet another contraction. "I wish my husband were here," she whispered through parched lips.

The nurse made sympathetic noises as she handed over a miniscule amount of ice chips in a paper cup. "I'm sure you do, honey. But nature takes its own course."

"WELL, WELL," THE DOCTOR said with a smile. "Aren't you the surprise."

Kate rolled her head on the pillow to look at her.

"There's nothing in your records about this, but it sometimes happens. Even after repeated ultrasounds during a pregnancy, we can miss seeing things."

Her heart abruptly lodging in her throat, Kate stared at the doctor and forgot to breathe for a moment. "Is…is something wrong?"

"Goodness, no—though you're going to be a tad busier than you thought." The doctor's smile widened as she looked over her shoulder and beckoned, and then Jared was suddenly there by the bed, wearing a blue hospital gown and cap, a mask loosely draped around his neck.

"Hi there," he said softly, his eyes warm with love and concern as he took her hand and brushed a kiss against her cheek. "Looks like you've had a big day."

It took a moment for everything to register.

She reached for him, then fell back against the pillows and looked at the doctor. "Busy?"

The doctor beamed. "There are *two* little ones waiting to meet you. It happens sometimes—a surprise to everyone. But we're going to need to take you up to surgery right away. There's a bit of a traffic jam going on, and you could labor until the Fourth of July and not make any progress."

Kate and Jared both stared at her in shock. *"Two?"* they said at the same time.

"An extra blessing, don't you think? But one of them is showing signs of distress, so we need to get in there and help out, STAT." The doctor nodded at someone standing in the doorway, and immediately, two orderlies came in with a gurney. "We'll use a regional anesthetic so you can stay awake, and your husband can be there for you. See you upstairs."

THE DELIVERY ROOM on the surgical floor might have been more daunting if Kate hadn't recognized a lot of the equipment and supplies from those she'd seen every day at the vet school. The friendly chatter of the surgical team added an extra measure of comfort.

The Minnesota Twins' win last night.

Fishing.

The hospital's annual employee picnic.

Then an abrupt silence fell.

The stainless-steel table was cold and hard against her back through the thin drape, but the intense expressions in the eyes of the surgical team, coupled with their ongoing silence, filled her with an even greater chill.

"Is something wrong?" She gripped Jared's hand tighter. She heard the panic rising in her voice and tried to quell it, but her anxiety exploded. "What's going on? Tell me!"

Another masked face moved into her field of vision and loomed over her. "You've got a beau-

tiful little girl who's doing just fine. You'll get to
see her in a minute. Your son is having a bit of
trouble, but they're transferring him to NICU right
away. Just hang on."

"Will he be okay? Is he all right?"

Above Jared's own mask, she could see his face
blanch and knew he was looking over the draped
curtain that had been set up across her chest to the
frantic activity taking place across the room.

And then, the activity suddenly ceased.

The world spun as she gripped Jared's hand, too
frightened to speak. Even before his soul-crushing
words, she knew that they'd lost their son.

CHAPTER FOURTEEN

PROPPED UP AGAINST A pile of pillows in her hospital bed, Kate stared at her new daughter in awe.

Until this day, every thought about her pregnancy had been tainted with worry about money. How she'd manage her vet school schedule in the fall. Whether or not she and Jared could make it through two more grueling years of school.

Who knew it would be like this—this instant, primal rush of fierce protectiveness and love? The unimaginable joy of holding this warm, feather-light bundle of soft blankets?

A perfect, tiny hand tightly clutched her finger, while those beautiful dark eyes were wide and fixed on her face, as if determined to memorize every detail of the one who'd brought her into the world.

Tiny, perfect toes, like small pink pearls, peeked out below the end of the receiving blanket.

Casey was the name she and Jared had agreed on if the baby was a girl, and the name seemed just right.

On a rush of emotion as swift and unexpected and overwhelming as a fierce summer storm, Kate's hot tears came again, spilling down her face. Uncontrollable sobs racked her body, sending deep, physical pain slicing through her belly.

One pink and perfect child in her arms.

The other—their precious son, Collin—had grown cold within her embrace not two hours ago, his life slipping away on a faint, almost soundless sigh.

The highest, most unbelievable joy.

Then, in a heartbeat, that joy had shattered against the razor-sharp rocks in the deepest valley of grief.

The agony of it welled up inside her until she could barely breathe, and she lifted her arms to snuggle Casey closer to her chest, needing the child's warmth as solace…though she knew nothing could ever replace the one who was gone.

"Do you want me to take her for a while?" Jared asked, his voice raw and his face so ravaged with grief that he was almost a stranger.

"No!" A keening wail rose in the room from a voice she barely recognized as her own.

He jerked back as if she'd slapped him.

"You aren't the only one hurting here." The sharp voice came from the open doorway and both of them startled at seeing Sylvia standing there, her face pale and strained, her mouth tight.

She'd actually come? In disbelief, Kate watched her mother-in-law come across the room to give Jared an awkward hug.

"You should have called me sooner," she admonished him as she stepped back. "This can't have been easy."

"It's been the best—and the worst—day of my life," he said wearily. "I don't know whether to celebrate or just sit down and cry."

"Let's take a look, then." Sylvia turned and took the baby from Kate's arms, pulling the blanket back to get a better look. "She's lovely. She looks just like your sister, except for the eyes—and those are definitely yours."

"But they're so dark."

"All babies' are, but they'll change. Just look at the shape, and those long, thick lashes. Most definitely yours."

The aching emptiness in her arms made Kate want to launch out of bed and snatch her baby back.

"It's such a terrible shame the other baby didn't make it," Sylvia continued, reaching out to rest a hand against Jared's cheek. "I'll bet he was just as beautiful. With a little more rest, less stress…

well, maybe things would have turned out much differently."

Kate blinked as the words registered, then sliced through her heart one by one, as neatly as any surgical blade. *Less stress. More rest.* Was it her fault that their son died?

She drew in a strangled breath as the implications settled inside her, threatening to crush her under a massive anvil of guilt.

Oh, God—what have I done?

COLLIN HAD SEEMED PERFECT in every way, and the autopsy revealed no specific cause of death… which compounded her guilt.

Had it been her lack of sleep?

Those endless, long hours of study?

The stress of striving for a top GPA?

The hours on her feet at the store, where she might've lifted too many heavy boxes, and maybe put some sort of stress or torsion on the umbilical cord, briefly depriving him of oxygen?

The reassurance of the labor and delivery nurses, her doctor and later her best friends about not taking blame for Collin's death did little to ease the piercing grief that dogged Kate month after month after month.

That dark, endless tunnel seemed to stretch

onward forever, offering no hope of ever reaching sunshine. How could it, when nothing in this lifetime could bring her precious son back?

As the weeks and months passed, Jared grew more silent, more distant, more tentative when he spoke. He'd been lost in his own sorrows, too... though his highs and lows never quite paralleled Kate's, so they retreated into themselves rather than turning to each other.

The first ten months had been terrible...yet they'd grown closer, too, in the dark of night, while sleeping wrapped in each other's arms.

And while loving Casey, playing with her, trying to keep up a happy front, so she could have a childhood with normal parents instead of ones who were mired in sadness.

Parents who looked into her sweet, beautiful face and also saw the son who was gone.

But now, with Casey's first birthday tomorrow, Kate took her out of the bathtub for their nightly game of peekaboo with the bath towel and realized—with dawning surprise—that it had been weeks since she'd had to turn away from her daughter to hide her tears.

Kate hid behind a corner of the towel, then popped out again, and Casey's belly laugh washed over her like a healing balm. "Are you Mommy's best girl?"

Casey threw herself into Kate's arms, laughing and planting damp kisses on her cheek.

"Looks like fun," Jared said, his low voice filled with amusement. "Wish I could play."

"You and I can play later," Kate teased. "When Miss Giggles goes to bed. But if you'd like to take her right now, it would be a huge help. Eight or nine storybooks would just about give me enough time to straighten up this bathroom and finish the dishes."

He stepped into the room and hunkered down next to Kate as she dried Casey with the towel, then put on her diaper and soft cotton jammies.

Even without looking at him, Kate could feel his warmth and catch the faint scent of his after-shave, and she felt a familiar tingle of awareness spread through her.

The moment she set Casey loose, the little girl raced to her toys in the living room, her chubby bare feet slapping against the hardwood floors, her wide-stanced gait sending them both into laughter.

"She is the light of my life," Kate murmured as she and Jared stood. "Maybe that pregnancy was a surprise, but I wouldn't give up one moment with her for all the gold in Fort Knox."

They fell silent for a moment, as they always did at moments like this, and she wondered what he was thinking. If he had regrets. If he longed for the freedom most of his law school buddies still enjoyed…without all the emotional baggage she and Jared still carried.

Collin's death had changed her forever, leaving her a far different person than the one he'd married in such a white-hot fever less than two years ago. Did he regret that now?

Jared wrapped his arms around her and pulled her backward against his chest to nuzzle her neck. "We're going to make it, you and me."

She closed her eyes and savored his warmth, the beloved feeling of his strong arms around her. "I hope so."

"That book we read said that losing a child is like the worst kind of 'trial by fire'—that it can end a marriage. I think it made us stronger." He kissed her cheek. "If we've gotten through this year, we can get through anything."

A brief image of his mother flashed through her thoughts. The subtle implication of blame Sylvia had laid at Kate's feet on that first day in the hospital. Her cool distance at the tiny, private funeral, when Kate had needed solace more than any time in her entire life.

"Even my mother," he whispered, as if reading her thoughts, and she could feel him smile.

"Even her." She turned in his arms and lifted her chin to accept his kiss. "I want to end up in rocking chairs together at some nursing home when we're over a hundred. I love you, Jared, and I always will."

CHAPTER FIFTEEN

Present Day

WHEN KATE REACHED the hospital, she hurried to the emergency department doors, nodded at the nurses standing inside and headed straight for the elevators.

She'd been silently praying the entire trip back into town, steeling herself for what might lie ahead. *Poor Casey, there all alone...*

And Jared—what about Jared? Why had she listened to the nurses who had encouraged her to leave for a while?

Upstairs, she strode straight to the ICU but stopped there, her hands braced on the door.

Through the windows, she could see the area was quiet. Several nurses were charting on the computers at the desk. Did that mean...

"Mom!" Casey came out of the waiting room to the left and launched herself into Kate's arms. "Where have you been?"

"I've been here since your dad was admitted. I only ran home and out to the clinic because the nurses said he was stable. Your dad…is he…"

Casey pulled Kate over to a chair and sat down, and Kate followed suit. "The nurses came out just a few minutes ago and said he'd stabilized, but we can't go in for another hour. He was in res…" She thought for a second. "Respiratory distress. Something to do with his medications and a coma."

Kate breathed a deep sigh and felt her tense muscles go weak with relief. "Thank goodness he's doing better."

"But if he's in a coma, will he wake up?" Casey's voice lifted in alarm. "Will he be okay?"

Kate gently took Casey's cold, shaking hands within her own. "He has a number of injuries. The most troubling right now is some swelling of his brain. That's why they dropped him into a coma with barbiturates—to help reduce the pressure. It won't be for long."

"I—I feel so bad." Casey swallowed hard, her head bowed. Strands of long blond hair had escaped her ponytail and trailed over their joined hands like molten gold. "I should've been here. M-maybe I never should've moved away."

"Oh, sweetheart. Of course you should have—

this is the time to spread your wings. You wanted so badly to go to school in Fort Collins, right?"

When she didn't answer, Kate freed a hand and reached over to gently cup her cheek. "I miss you terribly, of course. And so does your dad. But it wouldn't be right to hold you back."

Casey's head dropped lower. "Y-you didn't go so far away."

"Are you homesick? Has it been difficult for you?" That last phone call played through Kate's memory. The tension in Casey's voice. The hesitance. "If there's anything at all that you need to talk about, this is a perfect time. We only want you to be happy."

"I—" The elevator dinged softly, and Casey fell silent as footsteps came slowly down the hall.

Kate looked around, realizing now that the old man was gone. Her heart caught. Had his wife died? Or had she been moved to the cardiac floor instead? Or perhaps he'd just taken a short break, as well.

But it wasn't his deeply lined face that appeared at the door. It was Sylvia, looking ashen and weak. She was accompanied by a nurse, who had her elbow crooked firmly under Sylvia's arm to steady her.

The nurse frowned at Kate and shook her head.

"Mrs. Mathers has been discharged, against medical advice, and she refused a wheelchair to come up here. We tried, believe me. But—"

"I am perfectly fine. I'm going to sit right here, and I'll be far better off than I was downstairs on that blasted gurney." Sylvia's eyes flashed fire as she disengaged her arm and eased into a waiting room chair. "So just let me be."

The nurse gave Kate a helpless look. "We wanted to keep her a while longer, or at least arrange for transport home so she could rest. But she said she's staying at a hotel and refused to go there. Said she has to be up here for her son."

"I'll keep an eye on her. If we need any assistance, I'll call downstairs."

"That won't be necessary," Sylvia snapped. "If I get tired, I can nap here, or I can take my own car."

Kate met the nurse's eyes and gave a slight shrug. "We'll manage."

The nurse hesitated in the doorway, then mouthed *good luck,* before disappearing down the hall.

Casey sat back in her chair. "Hi, Grandma. Were you sick, too?"

"No, I was not. Just a little stressed, but anyone would be in this situation." Sylvia shifted and straightened her spine. "The nurses were quite wrong in ordering me down to the E.R.—

but I suppose that's how they try to bring in more revenue."

For a woman who "wasn't ill," Sylvia looked remarkably pale, and Kate wished she could run down to the E.R. and ask about her condition. There'd be no point, though, given today's privacy laws. She considered the best approach, and mentally crossed her fingers before speaking. "What sort of adjustments did they make with your meds?"

Sylvia pursed her lips.

"Did they order a stress test?"

Silence.

"An MRI?"

Sylvia's gaze shifted away and her lower lip quivered for just an instant, but at that brief glimpse into her soul, Kate saw her for what she was, behind the hard mask she always kept firmly in place.

An old woman in fragile health.

Alone.

Her only daughter away at school, her only son badly injured and lying in ICU—yet she was still too stubborn and prideful to welcome an olive branch of peace and comfort.

Decades of bitterness had carved those lines so deeply in her gaunt cheeks. And while Sylvia would probably never change, maybe it was time for everyone else to try a little harder.

"I know you aren't tired, and that you feel perfectly fine," Kate said. "But when you do want some rest, our house is closer than the hotel and no one is there."

Sylvia shot her a disparaging glance. "Thank you, but no."

"It would be quiet and peaceful, and the guest rooms both have comfy beds. Casey could probably use some sleep, too. How long have you been up, honey?"

Casey flashed her a quick look of understanding. "A good thirty-six hours, but I don't really want to go home alone. Unless maybe Grandma would go with me."

"Dr. Mathers?"

All three women jerked around to face the doorway, where one of the ICU nurses stood.

"Sorry," she said with chagrin. "I didn't mean to alarm you. If one of you would like to go back in to sit with Mr. Mathers, it would be all right. He's doing better. He's still asleep, but the doctor has tapered those new meds. And Dr. Mathers— you have a call on line four. You can take it in here, if you like."

"We should let Grandma go in first, don't you think?" Kate asked Casey. "I believe you must have seen him last."

When Casey nodded, Sylvia silently rose and left the room to be with Jared. Kate went to the desk phone on an end table to pick up her call.

"It's me," Amy said, her voice shaking. "I'm at the clinic and there's been more trouble. The sheriff is on his way over to see you. Tom, too, because he stopped in when he saw the patrol car out front."

What next? Kate took a deep breath. "I was in the clinic just an hour ago, Amy, and everything was fine. At least as far as I know." But had she looked that closely? Had the intruder been hiding inside, even while she was there?

"I was late for work this morning, because my truck had a flat when I got up this morning," Amy said. "I just walked in maybe ten minutes ago. The sheriff was at the café having breakfast, so he came right over when I called. Someone trashed your office—threw papers everywhere, then must've walked through your lab and pharmacy and swept everything off the shelves. There's broken glass all over. And this time…" She swallowed audibly. "This time, there was a note."

Kate felt her blood chill. "Do you have it?"

"The sheriff does. But I remember what it says. *'Back off or you'll be next.'* Next for what? And *why?*"

WHEN SYLVIA RETURNED from her five minutes at Jared's bedside, she looked even more exhausted. "His color seems better, and he gripped my hand just a little when I talked to him." She sank into a chair. "Maybe I should take that rest, after all."

Thankful for her change in attitude, Kate tossed the Bravada keys to Casey. "Can you bring my car up to the back entrance, so your grandmother doesn't need to walk so far?"

"I could walk," Sylvia sniffed after Casey was gone.

Kate nodded. "I know, but I just wanted a moment to talk to you alone."

The old woman's eyes flared wide with alarm. "About Jared? Is he worse than they told me?"

"No. I just wanted a chance to tell you how much we all love you…and how much I wish that there was a way to mend all the hurt between us."

Sylvia stiffened.

"I know you were against Jared's marriage to me. I know you had high hopes for something different. But," Kate added with a gentle smile, "we've made it for twenty years now. I love him with all my heart. And it would mean so much to both of us if we could all be a closer family."

Sylvia sat upright. Her rigid spine might have

been made of granite. But after a long moment, she turned her head away, her lower lip trembling.

"Please? You never know what the future might bring for any of us…or how much we'll need each other."

Sylvia clenched her hands in her lap until her knuckles whitened.

"I wish Casey could get to know her only grandmother better. She would love that. And it would mean so much to me if we could all start building some good memories…together."

Sylvia's mouth worked, as if she were trying to force words that just wouldn't come, then she turned away, her back rigid.

Ten minutes later, Casey appeared at the door. "I've got the Bravada at the entrance. Are you ready, Grandma?"

The older woman hesitated.

"Go on home and rest, you two," Kate said on a long sigh.

"You…you've been a good wife to my son," Sylvia managed after a long silence.

The words were stilted, still edged with ice, but it was a start. "I'll call immediately if there's any change. Okay?"

With a nod, Sylvia started to follow Casey out the door, then she turned back. Her face was still lined with fear and exhaustion, but there was a flicker of something new…as if those steel-gray eyes had softened, just a little.

Maybe there was hope after all.

JUST MINUTES AFTER Casey and Sylvia left, the sheriff arrived, his keys jangling in one hand with every stride and a scarred leather notebook in the other. Tom trailed behind, red-faced and breathing hard.

Kate gripped the arms of her chair and stood up. "The clinic has been broken into twice in twenty-four hours. Did you find any clues this time? Fingerprints?"

"I have a deputy going over the scene with a fine-tooth comb."

"I was just there—right at the clinic."

"I know. One of the deputies drove by earlier and saw your car."

"How could it happen so fast?" But even as she said the words, she felt a sinking feeling in the pit of her stomach. "I was being watched?"

"That's my guess. But it gets even more interesting than that." The sheriff glanced at Tom, then opened the notebook in his hand to review some notes. "When Jared's SUV was pulled out of the ditch, we didn't notice anything at first…as a lot of the paint was burned and the vehicle was badly damaged. And part of one side was buried in the damp ground."

Her sinking feeling turned into a cold, hard fist that tightened around her stomach as she thought about the dead woman and the evidence that might have been discovered.

"We think we found evidence that the vehicle had been sideswiped—there's some green paint residue. Do you remember you or your husband having any sort of minor accident when that could have occurred?"

"No. Never."

He nodded, his lips pursed, as if she'd just confirmed what he'd believed all along. "Then we can look at the possibility that a second vehicle was involved—either accidentally, or intentionally."

"And given the other threats, and the break-ins at the clinic, it seems likely that it would be the latter," Tom interjected. "I'm worried about your safety, Kate. And about Jared's, as well."

Kate drew in a sharp breath. "I just sent Casey and Sylvia home. Alone."

The sheriff tapped the microphone clipped at his shoulder and rattled off orders to a dispatcher, then signed off. "I've sent a deputy over there to keep watch, and we're having that paint sample analyzed to determine the make and model of the car that might have been involved. I also have a deputy questioning people in town to see if anyone saw a suspicious vehicle at your clinic this morning as they drove by. But in the meantime, we need to talk about the possibilities here."

Tom nodded. "The sheriff and I went through Jared's records at the free clinic, Kate. There are a couple that look suspicious—a large farming corporation accused by a neighbor of illegally contaminating Silver Creek with feedlot runoff. The neighbor guy came to Jared for help when the county wasn't taking quick enough action, I guess. There have been a lot of heated words— even some threats—back and forth between these two guys.

"Another case Jared has taken on is against a small meat processing plant in the next county. Two of the employees are trying to sue over being fired—unfairly, they say. Other than that, most of Jared's pro bono cases have been domestic disputes, or wrangles between neighbors."

She blinked, taking it all in. It wouldn't set well with those business owners if those little guys were now armed with a determined lawyer. Could someone from the corporation or processing plant have been desperate enough to attempt murder?

And were they determined not to stop until no further threat remained?

Tom rested a hand on her shoulder. "I'll keep looking through the records, and the sheriff's department is continuing its investigation. But be careful, Kate. There's someone out there who's wanting payback. When your husband wakes up, do everything in your power to make him back off from those cases for a while. Understand? *Everything*—before something worse happens."

"This is all just beyond belief." Kate said. "Twenty years of peace and quiet—then a car wreck, a fatality, and now these break-ins all at once." She shook her head. "Do you have anything at all on the woman who died?"

The sheriff flipped further back in his notebook. "No fingerprint matches. We found no personal ID on the body or anywhere in the car. There've been no missing persons reports that even come close. And without a list of possible names, dental records can't be tracked down for comparison."

"The labels in her clothes? Anything in her purse—a receipt, maybe?"

"Nope." He lifted a brow and gave her a piercing look. "Did you and Jared ever go out shooting? You know, target practice?"

"I don't see why—"

"I'd just like to know, ma'am."

"Some high school friend of Jared's took us out to a range a few times, but that was years ago. We shot his rifles and some handguns at targets, but we've never gone hunting. Why?"

The sheriff hesitated, his eyes still fixed on hers. "Because we found a .44 Magnum in the glove compartment of your husband's vehicle. Any idea why he'd be packing a gun?"

CHAPTER SIXTEEN

SPEECHLESS, KATE STARED at the sheriff and shook her head.

"Did he ever mention being personally threatened? That he needed to carry a gun for protection?"

"H-he never said a word." She paced a few feet away, then returned. "After the kinds of cases he's seen in court, he's always said that he's totally against people carrying weapons."

"Maybe he thought circumstances forced him to. Though I'm afraid there's no record of any gun permits being issued in his name…and that opens up a whole other set of problems here."

"I…" She fell silent. The free clinic wasn't in the best part of town, and who knew what sort of lowlifes frequented the area and might walk in for free legal advice? What did she really know about his life during those late hours? "I still don't think he'd ever buy one."

"He didn't buy this one. At least, not from any

reputable dealer, because the serial numbers have been ground off. What about the people he associates with? Do you know what they do for a living? Do any of them look dangerous to you?"

She felt a chill skitter down her spine. "Dangerous?"

"Guys who look like trouble from the minute you lay eyes on them."

"At the free clinic, maybe, but like I said, Jared has never owned a gun. I swear."

"Then why did he have this one in his glove compartment? There might be a lot of things you don't know about your husband, ma'am." The sheriff headed for the door, pausing there to write something in his notebook. "We've sent the gun off to ballistics."

"Ballistics?" She swallowed hard. "Why?"

"Because, Mrs. Mathers, the preliminary autopsy report shows that the female victim in his car was alive at the time of the accident, but it also appears that she'd been shot not long before. So if you suddenly happen to remember anything important, call me." His voice held an edge of exaggerated patience as he handed her a business card. "Here's my private cell phone number. Be sure to let me know."

WITH CASEY AND SYLVIA GONE, Kate took the next hourly visit at Jared's bedside.

"I'm here, sweetheart," she murmured, leaning over the bed rail to brush a kiss against his temple. "You're going to be just fine—I know you are. Once we get past this little problem, you're going to be on the mend in no time."

Sylvia was right—he did look better. His face now held a tinge of color, and when Kate gently squeezed his hand, there seemed to be a faint response. Still, his eyes didn't open and he didn't respond to her voice.

The hint of suspicion and veiled sarcasm in the sheriff's voice had played over and over in her mind ever since the man left, and even now she couldn't quell the tremor in her hands.

"The sheriff has some questions for you and I do, too, but it can all wait." She searched Jared's face. "I know you'll have an explanation for everything, and then we'll be able to get back to normal." *Please God, let that be true.*

She brushed back the stray lock of dark hair that always wanted to tumble forward over his forehead.

Explanations.

A word that had nearly triggered the end of their marriage when she'd demanded them long ago. A word that could spell even greater tragedy now.

She'd been so sure back then…so hurt and angry. Her suspicions had been fueled by stray gossip she overheard at the local beauty salon, and the whispers around town had seemed to follow her everywhere.

Someone had seen Jared with a woman in the next town.

Someone else had seen them holding hands.

At Casey's third-grade carnival, Kate had noticed two women laughing as another pointed out a tall, willowy brunette and said it was easy to see what Jared saw in her.

Kate had confronted him that night, and he'd lashed right back about trust and love, claiming he was equally hurt by her lack of faith and refusing to explain anything. After that, they'd argued more than they'd conversed, but eventually they'd both retreated into stubborn, frosty silence. Like a scab over a wound, it covered a raw underbelly of mistrust in their marriage for years.

They'd been excessively polite.

Excessively careful to explain five-minute delays or changes of plan.

Then gradually that faded, as well, and they'd been able to move forward.

Long afterward, the brunette spied them while they were Christmas shopping in Madison and rushed through the crowd to give Jared a quick embrace and a kiss on the cheek.

"Your husband saved my life," she gushed, turning to Kate. An immense diamond sparkled on her left hand. "I still can't thank him enough for how discreetly he handled my divorce. My ex was a violent man, but I couldn't be happier now."

After she flitted away, Kate had turned to Jared. "You couldn't have told me that? Wouldn't it all have been so much easier?"

"I couldn't"

"Not even your own *wife?*"

"Confidentiality." He'd shrugged, but she'd seen the turbulent emotion in his eyes at what his honor had cost him in his personal life. "It was a very high-profile case."

And it had been, when Kate thought back, vaguely remembering a powerful, philandering businessman, his socialite wife and his fling with a secretary. Eventually, the tabloids had made a field day of it, but Jared had never said a single word.

Now she looked down at him and prayed that his future hadn't been compromised by forces too powerful to withstand. "We'll get through this, sweetheart. I know we will. We have to, because you still owe me that last dance, and I won't let you go."

There would be a good explanation for the woman in his car.

For the weapon in the glove box.

Once he was fully conscious, he'd be able to solve all of the mysteries swirling around them. Then Kate could convince him to give up that free clinic and all those late hours, just as Tom had said, and life could go back to normal…safe and calm and happy.

Wouldn't it?

JARED STEELED HIMSELF against another wave of pain that had been relentlessly pounding through his brain for…how long?

The monotonous clicks and whirs of some sort of equipment went on, and on, and on. He smelled the sharp odors of disinfectant. Some sort of chemical. Where was he?

His stomach rolled, rebelling against the intensifying pain that seemed to radiate from every part of his body. *I've got to get out of here before it's too late. They'll come after us again. Just a few miles more…*

He tried to move and he couldn't.

Tried to open his eyes, to call out, but it was as if he were frozen in place, locked in a nightmare that wouldn't end.

Patty. Oh, Lord, where is she?

Alarm shot through him, cutting through the heavy cotton batting that had filled his brain, making it impossible to think.

Again, hallucinatory images assaulted him from all sides. Screams. Breaking glass. The smell of choking, acrid smoke and burning flesh. And then, like a miracle, he felt something real.

A cool, soft hand, as familiar as the beating of his heart.

A distant voice.

The faint scent of peaches.

Comforting, loving sensations. Only danger was here, too, looming fierce and dark—threatening to destroy everything good and wonderful in his life.

"Patty." He struggled to say the name louder, but managed only a rusty croak. "Patty? We…we've gotta go."

At a sharp, indrawn breath he managed to pry his eyelids partway open. Hazy images swam within his field of vision. Bright lights. Faces. Tubes and wires and some sort of silver bars fencing him in.

"Mr. Mathers?"

He blinked and the face of a heavyset woman in white came into focus.

"You're in the hospital ICU. You've been heavily sedated, but you're coming around. How do you feel?"

His throat was raw, thick. He tried to clear it, but that made it hurt all the more.

"You were intubated for a while, so I imagine your throat is pretty sore. Would you like to sit up a little more?" When he nodded, she touched a button to raise the head of the bed a few inches. "We're going to check you over a bit, and then your wife can come back in. She's been very worried about you."

He sank deeper into the pillow and closed his eyes.

She'd been here—he'd smelled her perfume, and he'd felt her familiar loving touch. Had he called out Patty's name aloud, or had he only dreamed it? Would Kate even come back in if she'd heard him?

He *had* to see Kate. Had to warn her, before it was too late.

But the lights started to dim, and he felt himself drift inexorably back into the darkness. He struggled to focus. To keep his brain clear…but quicksand seemed to enfold him, sucking him deeper into oblivion.

Please, God—keep her safe…please….

KATE PACED the waiting room, Jared's urgent words running through her thoughts in an unending litany. *Patty. We've gotta go, Patty.*

Patty had to be the woman who had died in the accident. But why had Jared sounded so urgent, as if they'd been fleeing?

Had they been running away together?

Kate discounted that thought as quickly as it surfaced. He was a good and loving man, honorable above all things. Whatever her first reaction had been at hearing the details of the accident, she knew deep in her heart that he would never just run off with someone. He would gently end one relationship before ever starting another.

So what did that leave?

A troubled client? But there'd been no record of any appointments the afternoon of the accident. Tom hadn't found any documents that could be associated with the woman who'd died.

A random act of kindness? Had Jared inadvertently become enmeshed in some sort of domestic dispute? But he wasn't a stupid man. He knew those situations were a great danger to the cops themselves, and he would've called 911 rather than playing the hero.

What else could it be?

And then there were the break-ins at her clinic. The anonymous, threatening phone calls. Was all of it related somehow—a plan devised by some angry defendant?

And what about Amy's flat tire? A coincidence, or had someone visited her place in the early-morning darkness to ensure that she'd be late getting to the clinic?

Kate shivered and wrapped her arms around herself, counting the slowly moving minutes on the wall clock, impatient for a chance to talk to him again. Should she share that name with the sheriff—or should she wait?

She hesitated, then left a message for Tom in case the name might jostle his memory. Finally she dialed the sheriff's private number. "I've got a possible name for you. Patty."

"Anything else?"

"Jared called out for her, and it sounded like he was in a big hurry."

"I've got a little news for you, too. The car that sideswiped his was probably a '98 Blazer. Ever had a fender bender involving that make and color?"

"No."

"Know anyone with a green Blazer?"

She thought for a moment. "I don't think so,

but I don't really pay much attention to what people drive."

"One other thing. My deputy found a newspaper delivery guy who claims he saw a Blazer parked about a half mile from your clinic this morning. He figured the car had broken down but didn't see anyone in it, so he drove on. We're searching Department of Motor Vehicle records for a car of the same description. Hopefully, we'll find just a few matches in the area."

She swallowed hard. "All of this could be connected."

"If it is, someone has a strong motive for revenge and was willing to kill to get it."

Kate's knees turned weak. "But at least Jared's safe here, for now."

"I wouldn't be so sure. A deputy is coming over as soon as he can, and I'd advise you to alert hospital security. If someone does come after him, he'd be a sitting duck."

SHE'D BEEN COUNTING the minutes until she could go back into the ICU to sit with Jared. Now at his bedside, Kate watched the wall clock's second hand make its way slowly around the dial. Security had been alerted to check all visitors coming into the hospital for anyone suspicious, but where was that deputy? Ten long minutes had passed without any sign of him.

Jared stirred. His eyelids fluttered, and then he fixed his bleary gaze on her. "Kate?"

His voice was just a rusty whisper, barely audible, but she'd never heard a more welcome sound in her life. She kissed his hand, mindful of the IV lines dangling from overhead. "Welcome back."

He lifted away from the pillow, winced and fell back. "I…have to tell you…"

"Shhhhh. It's all right. We can talk later."

"Patty—is she—" His voice strengthened. "Is she…"

He was so weak, so stressed. What was the right thing to say right now? "The woman in your car? She was…hurt badly, Jared."

There were so many questions to ask, she didn't know where to start. "The sheriff needs to talk to you when you're feeling better. He needs to know her identity."

"I'm…" He turned away, his voice defeated. "I'm sure he does."

He didn't offer further explanation. He wasn't even going to try, and she could already sense the distance widening between them. "Jared, look at me," she said softly.

It took so long for him to turn back to her that she thought he might refuse.

"The sheriff thinks someone intended to run your SUV off the road. He's trying to figure out who it is, so if you have any idea at all, you need to let us know."

The almost imperceptible shake of his head was nothing more than she'd expected if he still felt he was protecting a client's privacy.

"Maybe that person is still after you for some reason," she said.

His eyes drifted shut, closing her out. But she needed to speak to him before he did.

"We have to get some other things straight, too. I trust you, sweetheart. You've been my very soul since we first met in college, and I never should have doubted you. Not all those years ago, and not now. If that woman was in your car, you had a good reason, and I don't even need to hear it. Just get better, honey, so we can get you out of this place and bring you home where you belong."

Someone cleared her throat, and Kate looked over her shoulder to see the nurse had returned.

"He should get some rest," she said. "And there's also someone here to visit who seems awfully impatient, so maybe you'll want to talk to him."

Kate started to rise from her chair, but Jared's

hand caught hers and he pulled her back, his voice thick with emotion. "Stay," he whispered.

The nurse appeared at Kate's shoulder. "Sorry, doctor's orders, but we'll let her come back soon."

"I need to tell her—" He tried to sit up but winced and fell back.

"Whatever it is, it can wait." The nurse smiled as she picked up a syringe and injected it into the IV port. "This will help with the pain and will probably make you sleepy. Now just try to get some rest."

CHAPTER SEVENTEEN

SEVERAL TABLE LAMPS at the far end of the waiting room had been turned off. A man stood in shadows, his back turned to the door.

Kate felt a frisson of unease crawl down her spine. Yet hospital security had been alerted, and this man had made it in, so he must be all right.

If she wasn't careful, the next thing she knew, she'd be frightened by moonbeams and butterflies.

She ventured just a few steps into the room. "Are you the gentleman who wanted to see me?"

"Not you, your husband. I'm hoping you can help."

His voice held a false note of friendliness, and when he turned partway toward her, still in the shadows, her unease turned to foreboding.

"I'm afraid that isn't possible," she said. "The ICU allows families only."

"I just want you to tell them I can go in." He

bared his teeth in a chilling smile. "He'll be very happy to see me, I know."

The man exuded danger. She dropped her hands into the pockets of her blazer and found her cell phone, thankful that it had an exposed keyboard. Fingering its surface, she found and pressed the 911 speed-dial numeral that she'd programmed for emergencies. "I guess I don't recognize you. Are you a friend or a client?"

His shoulders twitched. "Both. Now can you go ask the nurses, or not? I'd just walk on back there, but they'd probably call in the National Guard, or something."

With good cause, Kate thought. Had her call gone through? Would the dispatcher's announcement also route through the sheriff's private number? If not, it could be a long time before anyone would figure out where she was right now.

"Okay," she said, forcing a smile. "Let me go ask and I'll be right back."

He turned fully toward her and loomed over her, one hand fastened on something bulky in his jacket pocket. With his collar turned up, his ball cap pulled low over his forehead and his amber-tinted glasses, it was hard to make out his features, but he definitely wasn't smiling now. "No. I'm coming along."

"It won't do you any good. I was just told to

leave, so no one can get in there for another hour. But maybe they'll let you take my turn, okay?"

"I can't wait that long." He shifted his weight from side to side. "Let's go."

She frantically searched for some way to stall. "H-how did you get past security?"

"What? You didn't know your husband has a long-lost brother? The fool security guard didn't even ask to see my ID."

If a stranger burst into the ICU, Kate had no doubt that the nurses would sound the alarm system in a flash. But even if they did, how long would it take for this man to reach Jared's bedside? What if he was the one who'd run Jared off the road, and he had a gun hidden in that pocket?

Stall him…find some way to stall.

"Okay…but I have to make a quick phone call to my clinic first."

He grabbed her arm and propelled her toward the door. "Not now, sister."

"I just have to tell my vet tech to…um…adjust the dosage on an IV that's due to run out in the next five minutes. If I don't call in time, my staff will call security to search for me all over this hospital." She managed a rueful smile. "They've done it before."

Swearing under his breath, he gripped her arm tighter. "Then make it quick. I don't have all day."

"Only if you let go. I have to get at my phone."

The man hadn't made an overt threat toward her exactly, but she could feel the waves of anger and beginnings of fear rolling off him.

She skipped the speed dial for the clinic and laboriously punched out each digit. She misdialed the number then started again. *Where were the sheriff or his deputies?* Had they gotten her first call? Didn't they usually follow up, even if the person didn't say anything into the phone?

Amy, ever efficient, answered on the second ring. "Kate? How's your husband doing?"

Kate closed her eyes briefly and willed the girl to listen carefully. "I'm here at the ICU, and he's not doing so well. He's going to need a *lot more help* in order to get out of here."

"What kind of help? Like more surgery?"

"I'm calling about that IV running on the Doberman."

"Huh? We don't *have* a Dobe here right now."

"I need you to up the saline to 200 cc's per hour, and start a sodium pentobarbital drip at 10 cc's per hour."

Amy fell dead silent for a moment, clearly processing the subtle message. "Are you in some kind of trouble?" she ventured cautiously.

"Exactly right."

"You want me to call the cops?"

"Absolutely. STAT. Thanks, Amy. I hope to see you later."

The intruder grabbed the phone from Kate's hand and turned it off. "Satisfied? Now get me in there. They'll bend the rules for you, and your husband will be real happy to hear what I have to say."

"Of course." She turned toward the door and upended her purse, sending the contents cascading to the floor. "Oops. Sorry."

She dropped to her hands and knees and began laboriously corralling everything, sending lipsticks rolling even farther away, fumbling with the shower of papers.

"Get up," the man growled. "Do that later."

A gut feeling told her that there'd be no "later" for anyone in the ICU area if she didn't think of something fast.

Her fingers closed around a safety syringe she'd absentmindedly dropped in her purse yesterday after using the needle on a splinter in her palm. Holding it beneath her, she unsheathed the needle and palmed the syringe to hide it. It wasn't much, but jammed in the right place it could be a distraction.

She kept reaching for her things, one by one, putting them in her purse, until he grabbed her arm and hauled her to her feet.

"Maybe I don't need you at all. This won't take long and then I'll be outta here. Loose ends are bad business, and I don't let that happen."

Sweat trickled down her back and her heart hammered against her ribs as she looked into his leering face. "Hear that? That's the elevator. People are coming. How many can you deal with?"

He licked his lips and glanced nervously toward the door. "I didn't hear anything."

"I did. Go now, and there's no proof you were even here. You've done nothing, so there could be no charges, no matter what I say. I'd just sound like some hysterical woman—and you'd be long gone."

As if summoned by her desperate, silent plea, a distant door crashed open and at least two sets of footsteps thundered down the hall toward the ICU.

He grabbed her, encircling her chest with one viselike arm, and hauled her next to him, then jerked a handgun out of his pocket and held it at her waist, out of sight. "If this ain't the cops, then we're going to walk right out of here and pay your hubby a little visit. If it is, then you're gonna be my ticket outta here."

The footsteps out in the hallway were closer now, slowing down. Tentative.

"Please—" She took a shaky breath, hoping they could hear her. "I don't want any trouble."

"One false move, and you're first," he hissed, jamming the muzzle of the gun into her ribs. "Your choice."

"Dr. Mathers?" The voice sounded like one of the younger deputies. "Are you having any trouble in there?"

"N-no."

He appeared at the edge of the door and looked at Kate and the man behind her. Awareness dawned in his eyes. He looked so young—too young to be taking a chance with his life.

She hesitated, then sagged against her captor's legs in a boneless faint. It would be impossible to imprison her with just one arm. The man cursed and stumbled back to free himself of her weight. With one fluid motion she rammed the full length of the syringe needle into the tender flesh at the back of his knee. He screamed and buckled to the floor, clawing at his leg. He threw the syringe across the room.

In a split second, the two deputies were on him. They jerked his hands behind his back and securely cuffed them. "Clark Porter, you're under arrest, and the list of charges is getting longer every hour."

They hauled him to his feet and started marching him toward the door. The older one looked over his shoulder toward Kate. "Can we get your statement down at the sheriff's office?"

She sank into a nearby chair, her own knees weak as jelly. "You bet."

"Thanks, Doc." He grinned. "Just remind me to never come up behind you in a dark alley."

CASEY ARRIVED just as the deputies were leaving. She stared at them, then spun toward Kate. "What happened?" Her face blanched. "What about Daddy? Is he okay?"

Kate debated about how much to say. "He's stable. And this was the end of a lot of trouble, I hope. Porter is apparently the man who has been threatening your dad and me over some legal issues."

"Oh, *Mom.*" Casey walked into Kate's arms and rested her cheek against Kate's shoulder. "You've been through so much. And I made everything worse, I know it."

"Sweetheart." Kate stepped back and held Casey's shoulders. "You could never make anything worse. I'm so happy that you're here."

A sob shook the girl's body. "I—I was sitting with him. He was unconscious, b-but I tried to tell him about…about something bad, and then the alarms went off and the nurses came, and he nearly died right there." Her eyes filled with tears. "I know he must have heard me somehow, and the stress—"

"*Casey.* He's *stable* now. He's doing fine. It was just a coincidence," Kate soothed. "If anything, your voice would've helped him get through that crisis. Believe me. You mean everything in the world to your father and me, and nothing you could ever do would change that fact. Understand? *Nothing.*"

Tears spilled down Casey's cheeks, and she shook her head slowly, her eyes filling with despair.

Kate led her over to the chairs in the far corner of the room and sat next to her, still holding her hand. "Do you want to tell me?"

Casey bowed her head, her silky blond hair falling in a curtain that hid her face.

"If we just get this over with, you're going to feel better. I promise."

"B-but it's Dad who's important right now, not me."

"Casey…" Kate gently lifted her daughter's chin. "Look at me. If you're in any kind of trouble, we'll do whatever it takes to help you."

"You and Dad both achieved so much in school. I knew I needed to do something really good with my life, too." Casey swallowed hard. "I didn't want to ever disappoint you. Especially since I got to live, and your only son didn't."

A chill swept through Kate at her precious daughter's revelation. Had she felt guilty about being a survivor all this time? "We would have loved Collin with our whole hearts, just like we love you. But you had nothing to do with his death. It was a fluke. You don't have to replace him or be anything different because he didn't survive."

More tears trailed down Casey's cheeks. "I—I just can't do it anymore." She drew in a shaky breath. "I wanted to go to medical school s-so you'd be proud of me. But I study day and n-night, and I still don't have a 4.0. And I—I just got my final grades back in chemistry and physics, and they weren't anywhere close. But I'll retake the classes, I promise. And I'll do better."

"Oh, honey. This isn't a tragedy. We only encouraged you because that's what you said *you* wanted." Kate felt her own eyes burn at her daughter's obvious pain and disappointment. "We want you to follow your heart, and do what makes you happiest. If med school isn't what you want, we wouldn't dream of encouraging you to try."

"R-really?"

"And the next time your dad wakes up, I promise that he'll say the exact same thing. Cross my heart."

JARED AWOKE when Kate returned from the sheriff's office an hour later. "I hear there was some excitement up here," he rasped.

She took the chair next to his bed. "A little more than I like, believe me. How're you doing?"

"Not as groggy." He nodded toward an IV stand that had been brought into the room while Kate was gone. "They've brought me a PCA pump so I can control the pain meds myself."

She reached for his hand. "I'm just so thankful to see you awake. Sylvia and Casey will be back in a half hour or so—they've been worried, too."

"Casey's here? And my *mother?*"

"And your sister's plane gets in late tomorrow morning, though she's on standby hoping for an earlier flight. Believe me, you gave us quite a scare. Are you up to hearing about it?"

Jared nodded. "I don't remember much from the last couple days. Just bits and pieces."

"Do you remember Patty coming to the legal clinic?"

He frowned, thinking back. "She wanted a restraining order and a divorce."

Kate nodded. "The sheriff has interrogated her husband. He found out that Clark had threatened to kill her, so apparently she came back to you yesterday, pleading for help to get to her sister's place down in Madison."

"I remember…" He rolled his head against the pillow in frustration. "I remember she'd been shot, but she refused to go to the sheriff or a hospital. Said she needed distance fast or she'd be dead for sure. She planned to contact the authorities in Madison."

"Clark confessed to breaking into my clinic and making the threatening phone calls. He was furious when he found his wife was seeking legal advice from you, and he was on a quest for revenge. He also confessed to shooting Patty and to running your SUV off the road. He seems to have a pretty strong policy about not leaving any witnesses alive."

"Careful guy."

"Until he wiped and ditched his unregistered throw gun after he shot her. That was the weapon she grabbed and brought with her. Another mistake was letting me make a final phone call to the clinic. Amy caught on and alerted the sheriff's department."

"Smart girl."

Kate could see he was wearing out fast. "I'd better let you rest."

"I need…I need to tell you something." He gritted his teeth and paled, then eyed the analgesia machine, letting the delivery push button drop out of his hand. "Things have been hard. My fault. I decided…you're right. It's not fair…to you. Not anymore. I'm closing the legal clinic."

These were the words she'd longed to hear for the past six months, maybe longer. If the clinic closed, there'd finally be a chance for them to spend more time together. There'd be freedom from the fear that gripped her heart whenever he worked there late at night.

And yet, it was totally wrong.

"You'd do that for me?" She'd been in love with him almost since the day they'd met, but now she felt that love radiate through her with even greater power, warm and deep and steady. A bond that would last for an eternity and beyond. How could she ever have doubted him?

He held her gaze with his. "It's the right thing to do. For us."

She shook her head. "I can't let you do it, unless it's really, truly what you want," she said quietly. "That place has been your heart and soul. It has meant more to you than anything else in your career, and I won't ask you to be less than the man you are."

"Come here." He glanced at all the medical equipment surrounding the bed and the tangle of IV lines dangling in the way. "If I can't hold you, I'm un-hooking all of this and walking out of here so I can."

The love and need burning in his eyes touched her the way no words ever could. Glancing over her shoulder to make sure there was no nurse in sight, she lowered the side rail and carefully negotiated her way past the IV lines and monitoring equipment until she could gently ease herself into his arms, for just a moment. The steady beat of his heart beneath her cheek and his firm embrace made her feel as if she'd just come home.

And just like that, they were twenty again—so innocent, so filled with the brash confidence of youth. So sure that nothing could ever go wrong when love was so absolutely right.

"We've had some hard times," she murmured. "But I wouldn't give up a minute with you to change any of it. It only made us stronger."

"I love you, Kate," he whispered against her hair. "More than you'll ever know. And I pray that your last dance will always be mine."

* * * * *

*Celebrate Harlequin's 60th anniversary
with Harlequin® Superromance®
and the* DIAMOND LEGACY *miniseries!*

*Follow the stories of four cousins
as they come to terms with the complications
of love and what it means to be a family.
Discover with them the sixty-year-old secret
that rocks not one but two families in...*
*A DAUGHTER'S TRUST
by Tara Taylor Quinn.*

*Available in September 2009
from Harlequin® Superromance®.*

RICK'S APPOINTMENT with his attorney early Wednesday morning went only moderately better than his meeting with social services the day before. The prognosis wasn't great—but at least his attorney was going to file a motion for DNA testing. Just so Rick could petition to see the child…his sister's baby. The sister he didn't know he had until it was too late.

The rest of what his attorney said had been downhill from there.

Cell phone in hand before he'd even reached his Nitro, Rick punched in the speed dial number he'd programmed the day before.

Maybe foster parent Sue Bookman hadn't received his message. Or had lost his number. Maybe she didn't want to talk to him. At this point he didn't much care what she wanted.

"Hello?" She answered before the first ring was complete. And sounded breathless.

Young and breathless.

"Ms. Bookman?"

"Yes. This is Rick Kraynick, right?"

"Yes, ma'am."

"I recognized your number on caller ID," she said, her voice uneven, as though she was still engaged in whatever physical activity had her so breathless to begin with. "I'm sorry I didn't get back to you. I've been a little…distracted."

The words came in more disjointed spurts. Was she jogging?

"No problem," he said, when, in fact, he'd spent the better part of the night before watching his phone. And fretting. "Did I get you at a bad time?"

"No worse than usual," she said, adding, "Better than some. So, how can I help?"

God, if only this could be so easy. He'd ask. She'd help. And life could go well. At least for one little person in his family.

It would be a first.

"Mr. Kraynick?"

"Yes. Sorry. I was… Are you sure there isn't a better time to call?"

"I'm bouncing a baby, Mr. Kraynick. It's what I do."

"Is it Carrie?" he asked quickly, his pulse racing.

"How do you know Carrie?" She sounded defensive, which wouldn't do him any good.

"I'm her uncle," he explained, "her mother's—Christy's—older brother, and I know you have her."

"I can neither confirm nor deny your allegations, Mr. Kraynick. Please call social services." She rattled off the number.

"Wait!" he said, unable to hide his urgency. "Please," he said more calmly. "Just hear me out."

"How did you find me?"

"A friend of Christy's."

"I'm sorry I can't help you, Mr. Kraynick," she said softly. "This conversation is over."

"I grew up in foster care," he said, as though that gave him some special privilege. Some insider's edge.

"Then you know you shouldn't be calling me at all."

"Yes… But Carrie is my niece," he said. "I need to see her. To know that she's okay."

"You'll have to go through social services to arrange that."

"I'm sure you know it's not as easy as it sounds. I'm a single man with no real ties and I've no intention of petitioning for custody. They aren't real eager to give me the time of day. I never even knew Carrie's mother. For all intents and purposes, our mother didn't raise either one of us. All I have going for me is half a set of genes. My lawyer's on it, but it could be weeks—months—before this is sorted out. Carrie could be adopted by then. Which would be fine, great for her, but then I'd have lost my chance. I don't want to take her. I won't hurt her. I just have to see her."

"I'm sorry, Mr. Kraynick, but…"

* * * * *

*Find out if Rick Kraynick will ever
have a chance to meet his niece.
Look for A DAUGHTER'S TRUST
by Tara Taylor Quinn,
available in September 2009.*

HARLEQUIN
60 YEARS
of pure reading pleasure

We'll be spotlighting a different series
every month throughout 2009
to celebrate our 60th anniversary.

Look for Harlequin® Superromance®
in September!

THE DIAMOND Legacy

*Celebrate with
The Diamond Legacy
miniseries!*

Follow the stories of four cousins as they come to terms
with the complications of love and what it means to
be a family. Discover with them the sixty-year-old secret
that rocks not one but two families.

A DAUGHTER'S TRUST by *Tara Taylor Quinn*
September

FOR THE LOVE OF FAMILY by *Kathleen O'Brien*
October

LIKE FATHER, LIKE SON by *Karina Bliss*
November

A MOTHER'S SECRET by *Janice Kay Johnson*
December

Available wherever books are sold.

You're invited to join our Tell Harlequin Reader Panel!

By joining our new reader panel you will:

- Receive Harlequin® books—they are FREE and yours to keep with no obligation to purchase anything!
- Participate in fun online surveys
- Exchange opinions and ideas with women just like you
- Have a say in our new book ideas and help us publish the best in women's fiction

In addition, you will have a chance to win great prizes and receive special gifts! See Web site for details. Some conditions apply. Space is limited.

To join, visit us at

www.TellHarlequin.com.

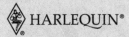

The Ranger's Secret
REBECCA WINTERS

When Yosemite Park ranger Chase Jarvis rescues
an injured passenger from a downed helicopter,
he is stunned to discover it's the woman he
once loved. But Chase is no longer the man
Annie Bower knew. Will she forgive him for
the secret he's been keeping for ten long years?
And will he forgive Annie for her own secret—
the daughter Chase didn't know he had…?

Available September
wherever books are sold.

"LOVE, HOME & HAPPINESS"

www.eHarlequin.com

HAR75279

In 2009 Harlequin celebrates
60 years of pure reading pleasure!

We're marking this occasion by offering
16 **FREE** full books to download and read.

Visit

www.HarlequinCelebrates.com

to choose from a variety of
great romance stories
that are absolutely **FREE!**

(Total approximate retail value of $60)

We invite you to visit and share the Web site
with your friends, family
and anyone who enjoys reading.

REQUEST YOUR FREE BOOKS!

2 FREE NOVELS PLUS 2 FREE GIFTS!

HARLEQUIN®

Super Romance®

Exciting, emotional, unexpected!

YES! Please send me 2 FREE Harlequin® Superromance® novels and my 2 FREE gifts (gifts are worth about $10). After receiving them, if I don't wish to receive any more books, I can return the shipping statement marked "cancel." If I don't cancel, I will receive 6 brand-new novels every month and be billed just $4.69 per book in the U.S. or $5.24 per book in Canada. That's a savings of close to 15% off the cover price! It's quite a bargain! Shipping and handling is just 50¢ per book*. I understand that accepting the 2 free books and gifts places me under no obligation to buy anything. I can always return a shipment and cancel at any time. Even if I never buy another book from Harlequin, the two free books and gifts are mine to keep forever.

135 HDN EYLG   336 HDN EYLS

Name	(PLEASE PRINT)	
Address		Apt. #
City	State/Prov.	Zip/Postal Code

Signature (if under 18, a parent or guardian must sign)

Mail to the **Harlequin Reader Service:**

IN U.S.A.: P.O. Box 1867, Buffalo, NY 14240-1867
IN CANADA: P.O. Box 609, Fort Erie, Ontario L2A 5X3

Not valid to current subscribers of Harlequin Superromance books.

**Are you a current subscriber of Harlequin Superromance books
and want to receive the larger-print edition?
Call 1-800-873-8635 today!**

* Terms and prices subject to change without notice. Prices do not include applicable taxes. Sales tax applicable in N.Y. Canadian residents will be charged applicable provincial taxes and GST. Offer not valid in Quebec. This offer is limited to one order per household. All orders subject to approval. Credit or debit balances in a customer's account(s) may be offset by any other outstanding balance owed by or to the customer. Please allow 4 to 6 weeks for delivery. Offer available while quantities last.

Your Privacy: Harlequin is committed to protecting your privacy. Our Privacy Policy is available online at www.eHarlequin.com or upon request from the Reader Service. From time to time we make our lists of customers available to reputable third parties who may have a product or service of interest to you. If you would prefer we not share your name and address, please check here. ☐

HSR09R

HARLEQUIN®
Super Romance®

COMING NEXT MONTH

Available September 8, 2009

#1584 A DAUGHTER'S TRUST • Tara Taylor Quinn
The Diamond Legacy
As if the news of a sixty-year-old love triangle wasn't enough to upset
Sue Bookman's life, Rick Kraynick wants custody of his niece—Sue's beloved
foster baby. And he appears to have designs on Sue....

#1585 HER SO-CALLED FIANCÉ • Abby Gaines
Those Merritt Girls
Only sheer desperation could make Sabrina Merritt tell everyone she's going to marry
Jake Warrington…before he even pops the question! She knows her ex hates her, but
Sabrina—aka Miss Georgia—needs Jake. And the governor front-runner needs *her*. It's
a win-win. Until their fake engagement turns into something more.

#1586 THE BABY ALBUM • Roz Denny Fox
9 Months Later
A lie is no way to start a job. Yet how can Casey Sinclair possibly tell her new boss
she's pregnant? Wyatt's still mourning the loss of his wife and unborn child. But as they
get closer, how long can she keep her secret?

#1587 SIMON SAYS MOMMY • Kay Stockham
The Tulanes of Tennessee
Dr. Ethan Tulane is in over his head. He's the new chief of surgery. He's learning to be
a dad to his adopted son. And he might have a thing for the nanny, Megan Rose. Can he
convince her this temporary gig could be permanent?

#1588 FINDING THEIR SON • Debra Salonen
Spotlight on Sentinel Pass
Eli Robideaux appearing in her store to "borrow" money is not the reunion Char Jones
imagined. But now seems the right time to tell him about the son they created—the son
who could be the missing piece of their lives.

#1589 HERE TO STAY • Margot Early
Everlasting Love
Elijah Workman thought he and Sissy could conquer anything together—their different
backgrounds, an autistic son, a house full of dogs. Then Elijah discovers their firstborn
isn't his son. Will the truth set them free to rebuild their marriage or will it ruin
everything?

HSRCNMBPA0809